HE WENT WITH

MAGELLAN

BOOKS BY LOUISE ANDREWS KENT

Novels

THE TERRACE

PAUL REVERE SQUARE

MRS. APPLEYARD'S YEAR

———————

MRS. APPLEYARD'S KITCHEN

Stories for Young People

DOUGLAS OF PORCUPINE

THE RED RAJAH

TWO CHILDREN OF TYRE

HE WENT WITH MARCO POLO

HE WENT WITH VASCO DA GAMA

HE WENT WITH CHRISTOPHER COLUMBUS

JO ANN, TOMBOY (with Ellis Parker Butler)

IN GOOD OLD COLONY TIMES (with Elizabeth Kent Tarshis)

HE WENT WITH
MAGELLAN

LOUISE ANDREWS KENT

Illustrated by PAUL QUINN

4039

HOUGHTON MIFFLIN COMPANY · BOSTON

The Riverside Press Cambridge

The Riverside Press
CAMBRIDGE · MASSACHUSETTS
PRINTED IN THE U.S.A.

For

SUSAN HOLLISTER TARSHIS

who went with

L. A. K.

CONTENTS

1. Noble Page; Noble Squire   1
2. Astronomers in a Garden   8
3. Letter to Malacca   19
4. African Ointment   28
5. Road to Spain   39
6. Long Days Waiting   51
7. Magellan Meets a King   60
8. Royal Contract   65
9. Alvarez   70
10. Turn of the Tide   80
11. 'Take More Ink'   90
12. Easter in Patagonia   98
13. Old Ships, New Captains   108
14. Nights — Dark and Bright   117
15. Rats and Leather   129
16. Spears and Javelins   146
17. Scent of Spice   155
18. Cape of Storms   163
19. First Circumnavigators   174
20. Message from an Emperor   180
21. Already Arranged   195

THAT DAY — a spring day in the year 1517 — began for Vasco Coelho like many other days. He was at the palace early, but not early enough for the schoolmaster, who scowled at him and picked up his rod with inky fingers. He was a little man and cross-eyed. This made it hard to tell just where he would hit you when you stumbled over a French word.

Vasco spoke French about as well — or as badly — as any of the other pages at King Manuel's palace in Lisbon, but his mistakes seemed especially annoying to the schoolmaster. Perhaps that was because Vasco Coelho did not care whether his long legs were swished or not. He had a way of looking through you, or over your head, with his dark blue eyes that made the schoolmaster turn red and stammer.

He stammered now as he said: 'And if S-Senhor C-Coelho would do me the favor to take his eyes off the harbor and t-turn them to the sonnets of Ronsard, a poet worthy of consideration even by those who esteem themselves p-poets . . .'

Vasco wrenched his eyes away from the Tagus. It was a ruffled blue and white that morning. The ships tossed up and down on it at their moorings and their flags and pennants whipped sharply in the strong breeze. White clouds blew over fast and made purple shadows on the blue water. The sun winked on gilded carving, on colored banners, on painted sails.

'Where will those sails go?' Vasco wondered. 'To Calicut? To Mozambique? To the Spice Islands? And I sit here,' he thought, 'reading French.'

'Swish, crack,' went the rod. Vasco looked thoughtfully at the welts that showed through his best stockings as if the marks belonged on someone else's legs.

Yes, this day was certainly going to be like every other day.

There would be the lesson in geography. The schoolmaster had learned it thirty years ago and had learned very little since. Vasco Coelho — whose godfather was Vasco da Gama, whose father had sailed to India with da Gama — knew more about geography than the schoolmaster, but he had learned not to say so. The schoolmaster still thought the world might very well turn out to be flat like a dinner plate.

Vasco knew how the morning would drag on. Music and dancing. Horsemanship. Swordplay. His fingers would slip on the strings of the viol. He would step on the toes of Princess Isabella's ladies-in-waiting and they would whisper to each other about his large feet. When he tried to mount, the horse would stamp and roll the whites of his eyes. After a while he would throw Vasco into the horse trough.

With the sword in his hand, things would be better. He could pretend he was on a deck that tipped and slanted under his feet. Yellow-faced pirates with knives in their teeth would come swarming over the rail and he would fight them till they fled to their junks...

'And if Senhor Coelho would honor us with his attention for a m-moment...'

Swish. Crack. More welts on his legs.

Yes, it was like the other mornings, except that the horse threw him into a rosebush instead of into the trough. Vasco picked the prickles out of his hands and went in to help serve King Manuel's dinner.

King Manuel the Fortunate was in a sour mood.

Probably someone has been asking him for money, Vasco thought, or perhaps the cook used too many eggs, or too much cinnamon.

King Manuel, being one of the richest kings in the world with the spice trade in his hands, wore a threadbare and motheaten gown of a style forgotten by most of his Court, and had an unpleasant way of nosing around the kitchen, hunting for waste. He paid his noble pages — moços fidalgos, in Portuguese — a few small coins a month and a certain amount of barley. You might eat the barley — if you could; or feed it to your pigs — if you had any; or sell it in the market — if anyone wanted it. If you kept on being a page for enough years, you might after a time become an escudeiro fidalgo — a noble squire — and get a few more coins and some more barley. Sometimes a noble squire might find himself on a ship going to India, and after that the world might be his. Or so Vasco Coelho thought, as he poured out scented water for King Manuel's greasy fingers. The King had just been smacking his lips over a small piece of roast pork. He threw the bone to one of his dogs. After King Manuel got through with a bone, a dog was likely to be disappointed. This dog, a white spaniel with a brown spot over one eye, chewed half-heartedly at the bone and then came and sat beside Princess Isabella's chair and turned up his soft pleading eyes at her, just touching the skirt of her dress with a silk-fringed paw. She slipped him a piece of meat while her father was not looking.

She looked more beautiful than ever as she did it, Vasco thought. She had warm golden-brown hair, the clearest and biggest blue-gray eyes, the sweetest smile, the loveliest fair skin, always changing from pale to pink and back again. If King Manuel had ever bought her any new dresses, she would have been the most beautiful princess in Europe, Vasco thought loyally. (He had not seen any others.) Even in her shabby chair, in the room with its dingy tapestries, in a dress made out of faded brocade that had once belonged to her dead mother, she was lovely enough so that some great painter ought to come from Italy and paint her portrait. There was a man in Italy called Bellini, Vasco had heard. One of the pages had travelled to Venice and had seen him at work.

'When I have my ship,' thought Vasco, 'I will bring back satin and velvet and fine linen, gold cord with pearls twisted in it, too. I will hire that Bellini — or that pupil of his called Titian they spoke of — and he shall get out his finest colors and put her on canvas...'

'You've put too much perfume in the water,' King Manuel whined. 'You boys will ruin me with your extravagance.'

He pushed his plate away and shoved back his chair. The pages began to clear the table. The Princess got up, swept her father a courtesy, which he noticed only with a small sharp movement of his hand, and disappeared behind a frayed curtain embroidered with tarnished metal. The red-haired lady-in-waiting, who was Vasco's cousin Angela Luisa O'Connor, looked back through the curtain and made a face at the King's back.

The big room was full of people who had come to watch the King eat his dinner. He was ready now to receive petitions. He generally granted those that cost him nothing.

He freed a boy whose father claimed the boy had been put into prison unjustly. Manuel often freed prisoners: prisoners eat. He granted licenses of various kinds: there were fees to be paid in return. He approved plans for carved doors for a church. These cost a large sum, but Manuel was more generous with large sums than with small ones. The thought of taking a milreis out of his purse made his fingers shut up tight, but he could promise to pay out many thousands of milreis in two years time with hardly a quiver. He could always raise the tax on cloves.

Perhaps if the short, sallow, black-bearded man who limped up to Manuel had asked for a large sum, things might have been different.

'Who is that ugly little lame man?' another page whispered to Vasco.

'Ferdinand Magellan — he came to our house once. He's been to Africa, to India, to Malacca, almost to the Spice Islands. He may be lame and ugly, but he's brave. I could tell you things about him . . .'

Vasco broke off because the lame man was speaking. He had a voice that seemed too big for such a small man. It was deep, not loud, yet it could be heard so clearly through the big room that the courtiers who had been murmuring and whispering to each other fell silent and listened.

'For many years, Sire,' Magellan was saying, 'I have been a member of Your Majesty's household: first, as is the custom, when I came here from Tras-os-Montes, I was a moço fidalgo. Later I went to sea in Your Majesty's service. I served in the East under that noble gentleman, Francisco d'Almeida. I have been wounded more than once, and lately in Africa the Moors have injured me so that I shall now go lame for the rest of my life. I have been shipwrecked and once I had the honor, in Malacca, to help save part of Your Majesty's fleet from the Moors. I was promoted to the rank of escudeiro fidalgo, with pay of nearly two milreis a month, some time ago. I ask now, Sire, for further increase of rank and to have my allowance increased by a milreis a month if I am to remain at Court. Or else, which I would much prefer, that I may take service in one of Your Majesty's fleets. Any service on sea or on land to which Your Majesty sends me I will perform loyally and faithfully. There is much of the world still to explore.'

King Manuel had let his eyelids droop over his pale eyes. He seemed to be half-asleep, but at the mention of the increase of a milreis a month in pay he opened his eyes and looked sharply at Magellan. His look had so much dislike in it that the courtiers began to whisper and mutter again.

'This request is impossible to grant,' Manuel said at last in his thin, sharp voice. 'If we increased the pay of every sailor who pretends to limp into our presence, our kingdom would soon be bankrupt. We acknowledged your valuable services, Senhor, on your return from the East, when we gave you the rank of escudeiro. More is impossible.'

Under Magellan's sallow skin, a dark red flush showed, but his voice was steady and courteous as he said: 'And my request for service as a captain? Denied?'

'It's denied,' the King said with that small sharp gesture of his hand.

'I have Your Majesty's permission, then, to seek service in some other country?'

'You have it.'

Magellan limped a step or two forward. There was a little wave of laughter behind him, and one of the courtiers imitated the limp. The King saw it and smiled.

Magellan, thinking perhaps that the smile meant that the King was, after all, relenting towards him, said, 'Your Majesty will, I hope, allow me to kiss your hand in farewell.'

'It is unnecessary,' the King said coldly.

It is difficult to limp backwards with dignity with smothered laughter behind you, yet Ferdinand Magellan managed it somehow, though his face was gray with pain and humiliation. He could not have helped seeing the snickering courtiers — there were two of them now — who were imitating his limp. He could not have helped hearing an escudeiro — a slender, elegant young man in puffed and slashed violet satin — say: 'It seems that lameness does not bring promotion. So, after all, my noble squires, we shall not have to cut off our legs.'

The young man had a very handsome pair of legs. He stuck out one and admired it and by doing so missed seeing Ferdinand Magellan walk for the last time through the door of King Manuel's throne room.

The King's astronomer had made a globe for King Manuel with Portuguese trading-posts in India and Africa and Brazil marked on it. The globe was on a table near the door of the throne room. It happened that the spring sunlight fell on the western half of the globe, on the bulging shoulder of Brazil, and on the coastline south of it that sloped away to the west. The astronomer had written 'Terra Incognita' — Unknown Land — on this coastline, and beyond it he had drawn an ocean full of sea serpents and mermaids. This was the astronomer's way of saying that he didn't know anything about that ocean either.

Magellan paused for a moment looking at the globe. No one but Vasco Coelho noticed the keen glance that Manuel's discharged squire turned on the Western Ocean: the ocean that, if you sailed over it long enough, would lead to the Spice Islands by a road no one had ever taken.

The motheaten curtains of the door to King Manuel's throne room fell together behind the small limping figure in black, and Ferdinand Magellan was forgotten there — for a while.

WHEN the King went to his room to doze happily over his account books, Vasco's duties for the day were over. He ran through gardens scented with red and white roses, found a door he knew, a door half-hidden by trailing vines, pulled it open far enough for a snake — or a boy — to get through, and was outside the palace wall.

Far along the path that twisted down the hill a black figure limped slowly through the dust. Vasco walked slowly too, keeping the figure in sight.

'What will Senhor Magellan do now?' Vasco wondered. 'He must be angry. Anyone would be.'

The boy's cheeks flushed as he thought of the King's cold, mean look, of the laughing courtiers, of the strange gray color of Magellan's face as he stopped near the globe.

'I must catch up with him, tell him I am angry that he has been treated so by those fools,' Vasco said half-aloud, but his feet moved no faster. He could not think of the right words to speak to a proud man who had just been laughed at in public, tossed aside by his King as if he had been a bone thrown to a dog — one of King Manuel's bones, already well gnawed.

Vasco moved forward so slowly that his feet soon ceased to move at all and he stood still, looking at the river and the bright ships. A new ship had come in and was lying at the end of the dock that belonged to his father's warehouse. Her flags were tattered by many winds, faded from sun and salt spray. Her paint was dull and dingy and much of the gilded carving at her stern had been carried away in angry gales between Malacca and Portugal. Men were unloading bales and bags from her hold. Vasco could smell cloves and cinnamon and nutmeg. The wind carried them to him and brought

the voices of the sailors. He could hear his Uncle Shane
O'Connor shouting directions. His Uncle Shane had a voice
like the wind itself, soft, but strong. Vasco could see him on
the dock. Shane O'Connor with his flaming red hair and bush
of red beard looked like no one else. Except that his daughter
Angela Luisa, Princess Isabella's lady-in-waiting, looked like
him — in the way that a young and pretty kitten may look
like an old cat — or so Uncle Shane said. Vasco had never
been able to see that his Cousin Angela was in the least pretty.
He liked red hair and freckles and green eyes on his Uncle
Shane, but for a girl they were a calamity. Besides, Angela
Luisa was always getting him into trouble.

'You can't really climb to the top of the grape arbor, Vasco
... no one could ... Oh, Vasco, how wonderful you are! —
I never saw anyone climb so high ... And since you're there,
throw me down one bunch of grapes, please, just a little one ...'

And then the gardener would come and catch Vasco among
the grapes and he would be scolded for eating them — though
he hadn't eaten even one — and Angela Luisa would have
disappeared, grapes and all. Certainly an annoying girl.
Vasco always promised himself never to be caught that way
again — and yet was always caught.

The tall old house — some people called it a palace —
where the Coelhos and the O'Connors lived was on the hill
back of the warehouse. Vasco could see the front of the
house and over the wall into the garden. The front door with
its bronze figures and the carved marble around it were new.
It was the fashion since Vasco da Gama had found the sea
route to India to carve stone with all sorts of fruits and flowers
and animals from the East. From where Vasco stood the carving around the door looked like a band of creamy lace, but he
knew its pattern of palm trees and monkeys and strange
flowers.

The flowers in their own garden were nothing but lilies and
roses and not at all interesting to Vasco. He could look down
into the garden and see his grandfather, old Abraham Zacuto,

who had once been the Astronomer Royal, sitting in the shade talking to a younger man. Vasco could see his grandfather's hands moving, so he felt sure the old astronomer was talking about stars.

Vasco's mother — she was Zacuto's daughter Rachel — was sitting beside him sewing silver stars and crescent moons on a new black robe for her father. Shane O'Connor's wife, Vasco's Aunt Luisa, was playing ball with her daughters and nieces. The game was to throw the ball and run to a certain tree before someone picked up the ball and touched you with it. Luisa Coelho O'Connor, in spite of some gray in her black hair, ran as fast as any of the girls.

It was only for a moment that Vasco looked into the garden. It was all too peaceful and familiar to hold his attention long — the rosebushes loaded with blossoms, the pretty pale-colored dresses of silvery blue, of soft rose, of dove color; the gardener working among the herbs, the butler bringing out a pitcher and a tray of silver cups. Yet the picture was printed on his mind. He did not know that it would drift before his eyes again when they were tired from icy winds or the light from a blazing ocean. He looked again at the dock. His father, Joan Coelho, a tall figure in black, was standing there now checking over lists of the cargo, and beside him was Vasco's brother, Abraham, that thin, serious model young man.

Abraham, Vasco thought, is the oldest and gravest of our family. How wonderful it would be if once, just once, he would do something wrong or foolish! Lose a paper about cloves or be late at dinner, or eat too many sardines.

But he knew Abraham never would. Abraham would always be glad to see the ships come into the Tagus full of silks and spices, and yet never wonder about the place they came from: content to see them sail and never try to stow away on one. Vasco had tried it and had been found and sent back before the ship even reached Belem at the mouth of the Tagus. And that had been his longest voyage so far. Abraham never hung around dirty little inns where sailors ate, and listened to their talk of storms on distant seas. He never thought that there were still places on the globe that no one in Portugal had ever seen. Or if such an idea occurred to him, he was quite willing to let someone else go and find out about them.

The names of Columbus, of Vasco da Gama, with whom his father had sailed to India, did not make prickles of excitement run along Abraham's spine. It did, however, excite him if a few pounds of cloves were missing, or if a length of silk was spotted with sea water. He took care of everything. It would be impossible, his father often said, to get along without Abraham.

Vasco could manage without him, however. He had meant to go to the dock and talk to the sailors. The sight of Abraham being so solemn and important made him turn to another path. His whole life, if he had known it, lay along that path.

It turned sharply, dipped down, turned again, and for twenty yards or so followed a level terrace. On this terrace someone with a love of the busy river, of ships, hills, and sunset clouds had placed an old bench of cracked and discolored marble. The man who was sitting on it now was not looking out over the Tagus towards the place where the sun was going down in a blaze of copper and scarlet and misty gold. His elbows were on his knees and his face was buried in his hands. Vasco, however, did not need to see Magellan's face to know him. He recognized the bristly black hair, the square, sunburned hands, the faded brown clothes, so much more like a sailor's than a courtier's.

Magellan heard Vasco's footsteps and looked up. Most of his plain, blunt-featured face was hidden by a bush of black beard. If you did not notice his eyes, he looked much like any other sunburned, bearded sailor. It was not only that his eyes were a changeable blue-green and seemed to see farther than landsmen's eyes. Many sailors have eyes that hold some of the color and distance of the sea in them. Magellan's eyes showed something else — pride, patience, an inflexible will.

If King Manuel, called the Fortunate, had looked into them, he might have saved himself much trouble, and — more important still from his point of view — money. For the sake of a milreis a month Manuel nearly lost his Spice Islands. It cost him many thousand milreis to keep them. It had been a mistake, he found out later, to sneer at Magellan's lameness.

Vasco met this stern, proud look. It made him think of a black panther he had seen in a cage in the King's gardens. Men had brought the panther from India and caged him, but they had not broken his spirit. King Manuel had not broken Magellan's spirit either, Vasco thought.

He said awkwardly, but so earnestly that Magellan's look grew gentler: 'Senhor Magellan, I saw you look at the globe. Take me with you where you are going. We'll show them — those sniggering apes. Noble pages! Noble squires! Noble lords! If that's nobility, I've seen enough of it.'

'You were there, were you?' Magellan said, looking up to Vasco's flushed face. 'You're how old? Fourteen? You look older; you're taller than I am already. I was younger than that when I left Tras-os-Montes and came to Court. I might go back there now, I suppose. There is a little village and vineyards. They make a wine that has a strange flavor — something wild about it. There's an old house with the arms of the Magellans over the door . . . on a silver shield three bars of checked silver and red . . . above it an eagle with his wings spread . . . Once I thought I would see it painted on my own flag, leaping from the mast of my own ship. I said that to Francisco Serrano. I will come, to you, I said, in my own ship with my arms painted on the flag.'

Magellan seemed to be talking more to himself than to Vasco. He looked out over the Tagus and went on: 'Yes. I might go back to Sabrosa in Tras-os-Montes. It's a wild place. The hills shut you away from the sea. In most of Portugal you're within reach of the sea, a short journey will put you where you can smell it and see it and hear it, but not in Tras-os-Montes. You boil there in summer and freeze in winter. They have a saying there: Nine months winter, three months inferno. Our fortunate King would be willing for me to go back to Sabrosa. He'll allow me to die quietly in that quiet corner of the world. He owns half the world, you know, because the Pope drew an imaginary line west of the Azores. Everything east of it belongs to Portugal: everything west of it to Spain. Simple, isn't it? Only — popes and kings may know where that line begins, three hundred and seventy leagues west of the Azores, but who knows where it ends — down under? Until someone sails around the world, no one can tell how big this globe is. King Manuel the Fortunate doesn't know where that line cuts through. He can't, sitting there pinching pennies, be sure that he owns the Spice Islands. And he doesn't know that — he doesn't know it ...'

Magellan stopped speaking and Vasco said in a voice that he could not keep quite steady, 'Is that what you were thinking when you stopped and looked at the globe?'

'Yes, it came to me then. I thought of my friend, of Francisco Serrano waiting for me, down under my feet, and the world seemed to swing over. I saw — as clearly as I see you — the Spice Islands west of the line.'

Magellan got to his feet and turned his sea-blue eyes towards the setting sun.

'I will come to you, Francisco,' he murmured, 'if not by way of Portugal, by way of Spain.'

'And I will go with you, Senhor,' Vasco said.

Magellan laughed — a laugh with more bitterness than mirth in it.

'I talk like a fool,' he said. 'No money, no ships. Cast out by the King. I might as well try to fly to the Spice Islands.'

'There are other kings, Senhor. Columbus tried Portugal; England. Then he went to Spain. By way of Spain, you said just now.'

'Did I?'

Magellan looked curiously up at Vasco Coelho. He saw a tall boy, much taller than himself, finely dressed in clothes of crimson brocade a little too small for him. Dark hair curled untidily over his forehead. His face was flushed partly with excitement, partly with the sunset glow. His dark blue eyes under heavy black brows had a look of loyalty and courage, Magellan thought. The boy's white hands and the feet in the square-toed velvet shoes were big and clumsy, but although his hands were white, they looked strong.

'Take him out and let the sun burn him awhile. Set him to hauling ropes with those soft hands, and he'll make a man yet. And he'll never make a courtier,' Magellan thought.

He said aloud: 'I can trust you, I know. I spoke too soon and said what I ought to keep secret, but I hardly think you will run back to the King with the tale. It's a new thing for me to keep secrets. I have spoken openly what I thought till now, but I can learn. Can you? If you can, it shall be our secret, but I wish you were an astronomer. I've sailed east from Portugal to Malacca, but I don't know yet how far it is around the world. Where West turns East again — that is still unknown to anyone.'

'I know two astronomers,' Vasco said, 'and they are both sitting in our garden.'

Magellan did not often smile, but he did so now.

'Why, this is magic,' he said. 'Who are they?'

'Look down into our garden. See, in the shade of the chest-nut tree, two men? One of them you know. He's my grand-father, Abraham Zacuto. I'm afraid he cannot help you much. He is very old now and he does not talk much except about the stars when he was young. The younger man's name is Ruy Faleiro. My father and my uncle think he is very clever. He had made charts for them. He is a man with a strange temper. Sometimes he is gloomy and angry and looks through you without speaking. Sometimes he is gay and likes to talk. He is a good geographer though people say the Devil makes his charts. Shall I take you to him?'

Magellan stood for a moment looking down into the Coelhos' garden.

'Yes, I will go,' he said, and after one more look at the setting sun started limping down the hill.

Luckily Ruy Faleiro was in one of his good moods. A globe that he had made himself was on the table beside him. The long evening was over and it was growing dim in the garden. Vasco brought a lighted lantern and held it over the globe. All his life he was to remember Ruy Faleiro's long fingers turning the globe; his pale face and Magellan's dark one bent over it; the light slipping over the curved surface; the names of strange lands coming into sight. After a while they set the globe back on the table again and the lantern beside it and went on talking. They had forgotten Vasco. There was no one else in the garden. Old Zacuto, murmuring about astrolabes that he had made and how he was Astronomer Royal once, had gone to bed.

The girls had all gone to sit at windows of the great hall on the other side of the house, because that was where young men came along playing lutes and singing. Their mothers were sitting near them to be sure that the young men devoted themselves to music and did not come climbing up vines to the balcony. That is, Rachel Coelho hoped no one would climb up because her niece, Angela Luisa, had come home from the palace and you never could tell about Angela Luisa. She might drag the young man and his lute into the room, or she might push him down and break his lute — or his neck. Either would be unfortunate, because, after all, a lady-in-waiting to the Princess ought to *be* a lady, Rachel thought.

On the other hand, Luisa Coelho O'Connor, Angela's mother, rather hoped there would be some climbing. And if there were, she wanted to see it. She considered that modern young men were very dull and tame, and she thought that her daughter was doing wonders if she acted like a lady even part of the time. Of course in a way it would have been convenient if her nephew, Abraham, who was so good and dignified, had been a girl, and if Angela had been a boy, but you

had to take the children Heaven sent you and love them.
So she loved them all, her own and her nieces and nephews:
good kind, dull Abraham; the tomboy Angela; her nieces
Maria and Olivia, who were so much prettier than Angela and
so much better behaved; her twin sons, Paulo and Dennis,
who were students at the University of Coimbra; and especially, somehow, her nephew Vasco Coelho, who was always
falling over his feet like a puppy that hasn't grown used to
his paws yet. There was something about Vasco's eagerness
to help anyone in trouble, his generosity and loyalty, something about his good-natured smile and his clumsiness that
made people like him. No one could help it. No one wanted
to help it.

Only it was strange, Luisa O'Connor thought, that Vasco's
father and mother wanted Vasco to be a courtier or a man of
business like Abraham. Anyone could see that Vasco was at
home only with ships. From the first time he sailed a toy boat
in the fountain, it was always ships with Vasco. He knew the
Coelhos' ships as soon as they came into sight far down the
Tagus. He could tell you just how many tons they carried
and how they were rigged, how their sails were painted. He
would spend hours whittling out model ships, and his clumsy
fingers grew clever when he painted sails for them. He knew
the name of every port between Lisbon and Malacca, and
could tell you just how much salt beef and biscuit you would
need for the voyage. He could describe strange harbors and
their tides and currents and winds — all as if he had sailed
there. He had never been out of Portugal, yet he spoke as if
he saw it all. There was a little boat he had sailed up and
down the Tagus, but if he had sailed her around the cape of
Good Hope he couldn't have seemed to know better the icy
storms that blow around the tip of Africa, or the hot rolling
waves of the Indian Ocean.

'Sooner or later he'll be a sailor,' his aunt thought. 'They'll
find it out.'

While she was thinking about him, Vasco was sitting cross-legged on the grass listening to Magellan and Ruy Faleiro. The lantern still burned and a swarm of moths fluttered about it. Sometimes a bat veered out of the darkness and swooped close to Vasco's head. The stars were bright now and the garden was full of the scent of roses. Outside in the street there was music. Vasco's fingers were too clumsy for the lute, and his voice was changing, but he loved music and there was usually a tune of some kind running in his head. Not the songs the other pages sang outside windows — songs about the silver moon and fair white lilies, or gentle doves, or sweet red roses. The songs Vasco knew were the kind sailors sing when they pull on ropes. The hymns sung on deck at night and morning. The calls sung when the sand has run through the hourglass and the new watch must come on deck.

'When my voice has done changing,' he thought, 'it will be loud enough to sing above the wind. They will hear me all over the ship, even when the ropes whistle and the sails are like drums.'

For a moment he felt himself carried out of the garden and down the river, saw the new tower at Belem shine in the starlight, felt the great Atlantic rollers lift the ship and foam under her keel, felt her stagger a moment, heard the shouts of the sailors, felt the sails fill and the ship settle on her course.

Above the noises of his imaginary ship, the delicious creaking and singing and splashing, he heard Ruy Faleiro say excitedly: 'It could be — yes, you are right — the line could cut east of the Spice Islands. They could be Spain's.'

Vasco looked up. Ruy Faleiro was bending over the globe again. The lantern threw strange shadows on his pale face. He wore no beard and his whole face seemed sharp — pointed chin, high narrow forehead, curved beaky nose. His eyes glittered in the light like the eyes of a chained falcon. His lips were pale, but he had bitten the lower one with his sharp white teeth and a little trickle of red ran down his chin.

'Hold the lantern,' he said to Vasco in a shrill voice. 'No, higher — no, you fool, not so high. This edge of the shadow must fall where I have marked it — west of the Azores. Can't you keep your hand steady, boy? The shadow must cut the globe in halves, not wander over it like the shadow of a cloud on blowing leaves. Steady, I say.'

'Your own hand is shaking, Senhor Faleiro,' Vasco heard Magellan say quietly. 'Let me take the globe.'

The globe passed from Faleiro's long pale fingers to Magellan's stubby brown ones.

Now one edge of the shadow touched the place that Faleiro had marked — that imaginary line three hundred and seventy leagues west of the Azores. And on the other side of the world within the lighted half of the globe lay the Spice Islands . . .

The lantern began to flicker. It went out and the smell of the dying wick choked out the smell of the roses. Vasco's eyes were still dazzled by looking at the lighted globe, so he never knew how Magellan looked as he said, still in that quiet, calm voice: 'If your globe is the right size, Senhor Faleiro, if the western ocean is as you have drawn it, the Spice Islands lie in Spanish territory.'

Faleiro said angrily: 'I do not make mistakes in my charts. Men have sailed by them to ——' Here he reeled off a long list of foreign names, and followed them with a flood of figures and astronomical calculations, and wound up: 'And if this big fool had held the light steady and not let it go out, you would have seen.'

Magellan had listened patiently. He had put down the globe and at the word 'fool' he put his hand on Vasco's arm. It seemed as if patience and determination flowed from his fingers.

'The way to be sure,' he said calmly, 'will be to go and look.'

LETTER TO MALACCA ————————————

THAT evening in the garden was only the first of those that Vasco spent with Magellan and Ruy Faleiro. Magellan lived at a small inn near the docks. It was to his hot, dingy room, close under the roof, that Vasco used to go after his day at the palace was over. Vasco could write clearly and spell after his own fashion. It seemed to satisfy Magellan, who hated to cramp his fingers around a pen. More and more the boy came to act as Magellan's secretary, writing down for him long lists of supplies that would be needed to sail to — some place not mentioned, a two years' voyage away, copying out pages about latitude and longitude, about tides and winds, making copies of agreements between the astronomer and Magellan, and watching Faleiro tear them up again.

As the summer dragged on and the smells of the river and the city grew heavier, Vasco came more and more to dislike Ruy Faleiro. Faleiro would be sunk in gloom one evening and would refuse to speak. When he did speak, it would be to prophesy disaster on land and sea. The next night, perhaps, he would be gay and friendly, giving valuable information so fast that Vasco's pen could not keep up with it, telling jokes and laughing at them, singing foolish songs with tunes that kept on dancing in Vasco's head all night when he should have been asleep. Another evening Faleiro would still be talkative but quarrelsome and suspicious, accusing Magellan of planning to use Faleiro's secret way of figuring longitude to cheat him out of the profits of the voyage.

It began to seem to Vasco that the people in Lisbon who said that the Devil made Faleiro's charts for him were right. When the astronomer's pale yellow-brown eyes glittered in the candlelight as he glared at Magellan and accused him of treachery, when his pale dirty fingers clawed into pieces some paper that Vasco had written, when Faleiro sat muttering to himself, or to someone just over his shoulder, someone no one else could see, it seemed that there was indeed an evil spirit crowded into the stuffy little room with them.

All through Faleiro's changes of mood Magellan remained the same, quiet and patient, yet with a kind of stern obstinacy over which Faleiro's waves of temper broke like the tide breaking over a hidden rock. The rock let the waves boil up around it, but when the tide went down the rock was still there, dark, solid, unmoved.

At first it had been partly curiosity about anyone who had sailed to the mysterious East, partly pity because of the way Magellan had been treated by King Manuel, that drew Vasco to Magellan. The curiosity continued. As long as there was anything a sailor could tell him, Vasco would listen. This had been so since he had been just big enough to sit on a coil of rope on his father's dock and watch a loaded ship slip down the Tagus into the wind.

The pity, however, was soon gone. Magellan might be poor, ugly, lame, out of favor with his King, but pity is for the weak, and this blunt-faced unsmiling little man was strong.

One hot August evening Magellan and Vasco were alone except for Magellan's Malay servant. Faleiro had left in a fit of anger the night before because Magellan had said, in Vasco's hearing, that Faleiro and Magellan must publicly give up their Portuguese citizenship and become citizens of Spain —

or of any other country that would give them ships for the Spice Islands.

Faleiro had raged up and down the little room calling Magellan names in his shrill harsh voice.

'Now this young Coelho knows our secret. He will run and tell his father — run and tell the King. He's a traitor. I see it in his eyes. Why have you had him here to spy on us? He will tell the King and we shall be arrested. Why did you let him hold the lantern that night? He knows where the shadow fell.'

There was more, much more, of this talk, but Magellan at last succeeded in stopping it. Faleiro changed from rage to sulky gloom. He had gone away still sulking, and this evening had not appeared.

Faleiro had torn more papers, his favorite gesture when angry, the night before, and Vasco had set to work quietly to make new copies. It was hotter than ever that evening and the sweat trickled down Vasco's nose as he wrote. He kept wiping his forehead with the back of his hand, but that was wet, too, and somehow he managed to get some smears of ink on his face.

Magellan sat by the window. He had a chessboard on a table in front of him and was playing a game against himself. The pieces were of carved ivory, some a creamy white and some dyed a bright red that was neither scarlet nor crimson. The juice of ripe cherries on snow might look like that, Vasco thought.

'Did you bring the chessmen from India?' Vasco asked, putting down his pen and making more ink smears on his face.

Magellan picked up one of the pieces and handed it to Vasco. It was an elephant with a castle on his back. Like the other pieces, the elephant stood on a base that bulged out into a carved ball. There was another ball carved inside the first one and a third ball no bigger than a pea carved inside that. If you shook it even a little, you could hear them rattle against each other and see the balls move. On the board there were foot soldiers with swords, and knights with spears. The queens were tall with flowing robes. They carried half-opened fans. The kings were fat and important and their clothes were magnificently embroidered. The bishops had their hands folded. They looked wisely down their flat noses with their slanted eyes.

'Not from India,' Magellan said. 'It is Chinese work. I found it — that is, it was given to me — in Malacca.'

At the word 'Malacca' there was a stir in the corner of the room. The Malay servant, Enrique, had been lying asleep on a piece of matting. Enrique was a tall brown-faced man with blue-black hair. He shook his hair out of his eyes as he got up, and said, speaking in Portuguese: 'Tell him, Senhor, how you got the chessmen.'

Magellan shrugged his shoulders and shook his head.

'Then I will tell,' said Enrique.

He sat cross-legged on his mat, speaking rather slowly, pausing for a word now and then. His voice was pleasant and soft. It made Vasco think of harbors scented with spice, of ships with sails of matting sliding through green water, of the sound of tinkling bells blown across a brown river.

'The city of Malacca stretches far along the shore,' Enrique said. 'There were Persians and Arabs, Chinese, men from the distant Spice Islands trading in its busy markets that day. They were all angry when the ships came from Portugal. The King was afraid. He plotted to seize the ships and kill the strangers.

'First he invited them all to a feast on shore, but the Captain — I forget his name ——'

'Sequeira,' Magellan said quietly.

'I thank you, Senhor. This Captain Sequeira he was too wise — at first. Then some days go by. He forgets to be so wise. He is a big, jolly man, a little lazy. Then the King sends some fine presents — chickens, fruit, silks, chessmen. He has found out that the Captain will sit for hours over a chessboard forgetting time. Also, the King says, there is a big cargo ready for the Portuguese — much pepper, much spice. He says the wind, the east monsoon, will come soon and blow them home again. He says the Captain must send his boats ashore quickly for the cargo. Then the ships will be loaded and ready when the monsoon blows. The King also sent some fine messages. I was one of the eight men who went to the ship. I went to speak the King's words in Portuguese. I had learned it in India. Our leader spoke in our tongue first. Then I spoke in Portuguese.'

'Were you not afraid of the strange weapons on the ships — the guns, the cannon?' Vasco asked.

Enrique stood up and took from the wall a carved sheath of brown wood. Out of it he pulled a wavy-bladed Malay kris. It was in his hand so fast that the movement seemed only a flash of light that ran along the scalloped edge of the broad blade and sparkled at the sharp point.

'We had these,' he said. 'Our orders were to strike when we saw a puff of smoke from the Citadel. If it had not been for Senhor Magellan ——'

Magellan said with one of his rare smiles: 'Enrique likes to make a good story out of a very simple matter. There was a little delay, but we got safely out of the harbor and the monsoon blew us home — that's all.'

'Please, Senhor, I should like to hear Enrique tell it,' Vasco said.

'Very well. Go on, Enrique.'

Magellan yawned and moved a knight two squares forward and one to the left, and Enrique went on: 'We found Captain Sequeira playing chess with the ship's doctor and nearly asleep over the board — or so he looked till the doctor took the Captain's white queen with one of his red knights, and then he woke up and was angry. When he heard the cargo was ready he ordered the boats ashore and went on scowling over the board.

'Now, Senhor Magellan did not go ashore. He had seen the people from the city flocking to the ships to trade. He suspected that the King meant to fill the ships with his men and then seize them while the boats were ashore. He told the captain of his ship — Captain da Sousa — what he suspected. Da Sousa sent him to warn Captain Sequeira.

'We were still standing around Captain Sequeira watching him lose his game of chess when Senhor Magellan came over the side and walked up to the players. He did not know I understood him and he said, "There is treachery afoot, be on your guard," but the fat captain only went on looking at the chessboard as if he had not heard.

'Senhor Magellan went away then. I could hear his angry feet going fast on the deck. It was before my master got the wound in his knee. He could move like a bird then.'

Enrique dropped his voice, although Magellan did not seem to be listening. He was as intent over his chessboard as Captain Sequeira had been on that hot afternoon in Malacca.

'One of our men half-drew his kris, but our leader motioned to him not to strike. We stood there quietly watching for the puff of smoke. Suddenly I saw some Portuguese sailors running down the beach. I knew one of them. I had seen him with Captain Magellan in the city. His name was Francisco Serrano — a tall man with hair and beard like raw silk and eyes like bright sapphires and a great voice like a strong wind blowing.

'He called Senhor Magellan's name, and with one last cry of "Treachery! Treachery!" Senhor Magellan started rowing for the beach. Captain Sequeira heard him and jumped up, knocking over the chessboard — see, one of the white knights still has a broken lance. Our leader struck at him. The kris missed him by the breadth of a fingernail. Just then the puff of smoke came from the Citadel, but it was too late for us. Sailors came running at us. They were too many for us. All but I jumped into the sea and swam for shore. One of the sailors had knocked my kris out of my hand and was stabbing at me with his knife. Others threw me to the deck. They bound me with ropes and tied me to the mast, so that my feet could not touch the deck.

'I could see Senhor Serrano in a small boat, rowing like mad for his ship, and our people in boats chasing him. Soon they were all around him. Two of them jumped on board and stabbed one of the men who was with him. Just then Senhor Magellan got there. He had only four men with him but they fought like demons, upsetting boats, jumping from one boat to the next, slashing and cutting about them with their swords. Soon there was open water around Serrano's boat Our people fled back to the shore.

'Senhor Magellan and Senhor Serrano brought their wounded men back to our ship, for there was still fighting on the other ships of our fleet. Captain Sequeira's servant was picking up the chessmen from the deck and putting them in the box when they came.

'The fat Captain spoke gratefully to Senhor Magellan.

'"If it were not for you, Senhor," he said, "my head might now be separated from my body. So what can I do for you, Senhor?"

'Then, before he got his answer, he said to the servant: "I swear I'll never play another game of chess. Throw that box into the water." Only Senhor Magellan laughed and said, "No, give them to me. I'll keep them to remember this day."

'He could have asked for money or promotion, you see,' said Enrique, speaking softly, 'but — he only asked for something that was to be thrown away. He said, "I will come back for them later. Just now I have business."

'Then he set the box on the table and he and Senhor Serrano rowed back to their own ship, for again there was fighting around it. I could hear Senhor Serrano across the water shouting and laughing as he fought and see Senhor Magellan's sword flashing and see him move as fast as a black-and-red dragonfly. He wore black and red that day.

'Then Sequeira's ship began to move and the cannon were fired. In the smoke of the battle, I saw no more of Senhor Magellan. I thought I should be killed or die of thirst bound to that mast. My wounds were still bleeding. At last our people were frightened away by the cannon and their boats were sunk. It was all over.

'The Portuguese sailed with the monsoon, though without the cargo of spices they had hoped for. And I sailed with them.'

'Still bound to the mast?' Vasco asked.

'No. Senhor Magellan came back for his chessmen. I was still hanging there. I spoke to him in Portuguese — asked him for water. He was angry with the sailors who had tied me there — he is a stern man, my master, but not cruel. I could not understand all he said to the sailors — I was weak with thirst and from my wounds and from the sun blazing on my head and the smoke of the guns. The words ran together too fast for me, but I remember Senhor Magellan's tossing some pieces of gold to the sailor, and afterwards I learned that the sailor planned to sell me in Portugal.

'So they cut me down and Senhor Magellan picked up the chessmen with one hand and threw me over his shoulder, though I am tall and no light weight. We went back to his ship. Since then I have been his slave.'

Enrique's voice rose a little. It reached Magellan's ears, roused him from the half-dream in which he had been sitting, looking sometimes at the moonlit river and at the dark ships with their faintly gleaming lanterns, and sometimes at the chessboard with its delicately carved kings and queens.

'Enrique means that I am his slave,' he said gravely, but with a twinkle in his eyes. 'I wear what he tells me to, eat what he says is good for me, get up and go to sleep at his orders. Enrique is homesick, so I am going to try to sail around the world and take him back to Malacca. Certainly I am the slave, not Enrique. And when I die ——'

Here the Malay broke in, talking in his own language.

'He says I must not speak of it — that it is bad luck,' Magellan said, 'so I will only say — for you must write it for me some day, Vasco — that by my will he is to have his freedom. He says also that I have played chess enough and that *I* must sleep now and that he will see you home, because we have talked too long and it is late. I told you I was the slave. We must do as he says.'

Yet though Magellan had his orders he did not lie down on the bag of mouldy straw that was his bed. There was still oil left in the lamp and by its smoky, flickering light he wrote a letter to his friend, Francisco Serrano, the man whose life he had twice saved, once in the sea fight off Malacca, again in a shipwreck near Mozambique. Serrano had written to say that Magellan must come to the Spice Islands.

Magellan took the letter from his pouch and looked at it again. He did not read it. He knew it by heart — even the figures about the price of cloves — but he looked again at the last sentence.

'I am here,' his friend had written, 'waiting for you.'

Magellan thought of Francisco with his big, gay laugh, his eyes like distant mountains on a clear day. He remembered how Francisco would take a step or two on his toes before he would draw his sword and leap aside from a hostile blade as quickly as a cat. He remembered how Francisco had made them all laugh when they were wrecked on a sandbank. Thinking of Serrano made the pen slip easily over the paper.

'I will come to you, Francisco,' he wrote, 'if not by way of Portugal, by way of Spain.'

AFRICAN OINTMENT ———————— 4

OUTSIDE the tavern the street was like a hot, black tunnel. The old houses seemed to tip in towards each other. A heavy cloud had blotted out the moon. No light shone in the narrow slit of sky above them.

Enrique muttered: 'A fine place to get a knife between the ribs. I have kept you too late. Let me go first, Senhor. I know the way.'

Vasco followed the Malay's tall figure. Enrique wore white. In this darkness he was a pale gray shadow of a man. Where the street twisted into another as dark and narrow, there was a gleam of light. There was another tavern there. The sign had a red cat painted on it, Vasco remembered.

'Someone awake at the Red Cat,' Enrique said softly. 'I would rather pass here at noon than at night. More than one man has gone in there and next morning waked up on a ship sailing for the end of the earth.'

'Wouldn't you be glad to sail to Malacca?'

'Not so loud, Senhor ... Yes, with my master. But not without him, and to some land of ice. Why, in the north there are deer with horns of ice. They pierce you with horns and freeze you, I have heard, and the savages who own them keep you on ice till they are ready to eat you.'

Enrique whispered this information and shivered in spite of the airless heat.

'Wait,' he added, and moved forward.

The light from the Red Cat threw a pink glow on his white clothes. Suddenly he stumbled and fell. There was more light from the door of the tavern. Two figures were dark against it. Vasco ran forward. He saw a rope stretched across the street.

'That was why he fell,' he thought, and jumped over it, jerking his sword out of the scabbard.

The two men who were dragging Enrique towards the door looked up and saw a figure in red with red light flashing along the drawn sword. One of them dropped Enrique's feet and ran. The other was braver. He dropped the Malay's shoulders and stabbed at Vasco with a dagger, but then ran bellowing as the sword pricked him in the arm. Enrique was on his feet now and his Malay kris was out of its wooden sheath. The door of the Red Cat banged against the point. Inside a heavy bar thumped into place.

Through the thick door Vasco heard a voice shout: 'I tell you it was the Devil himself in scarlet with a sword seven feet long and red hot at the end. It scorched me, I tell you. Catch men for your crew yourself.'

A hoarse voice roared: 'Don't be a fool, Pedro. Six of you go and find these men before they tell this all over the city.'

'We had better go,' Enrique said. 'Can you help me, Senhor? They have given my ankle a twist with that rope of theirs and something makes me dizzy.'

'I'll take you home with me,' Vasco said. 'We are nearer my house than yours and with safer streets for walking.'

He cut the rope and coiled it up quickly.

'This won't catch any more sailors,' he said. 'I'll save it in case I meet our friends and a tree to hang them on. Put your arm around my neck, Enrique.'

There were still lights in the Coelhos' house — lights and music and the smell of hot food.

'I forgot,' Vasco said. 'It is the feast for my cousin's betrothal. Now I shall be scolded for being late, but it won't be
the first time. Don't worry, Enrique.'

Enrique, who had fainted, was not worrying.

Maria da Sousa never forgot the night when she first saw
Vasco Coelho. She had come that week from the convent and
this was her first day as one of Princess Isabella's ladies-in-
waiting. Her brother Christoval, the young Marquis, was
being betrothed to Angela Luisa O'Connor. The Princess
and all her ladies had come to the feast.

It was, after all, the tomboy Angela, Angela with the red
hair, who was to be married before any of her pretty cousins.
Christoval had come home from India, had seen Angela at
Court twice, and had fallen in love with her. The families
had long been friends. Indeed Maria's guardian was Joan
Coelho. Only she had been in the convent since her parents
died when she was hardly more than a baby, so she had not
seen the young Coelhos and O'Connors since they grew up.

This had been the most exciting day of Maria's life. She
loved everything — the music, the food, Angela's red hair.

'I wish I had red hair,' she thought. 'No one would even
look at me twice. I am too small and my nose is too short.
What a lovely nose the Princess has! — so straight. And her
hair catches the candlelight and her eyes are like lakes in the
spring sunshine. She is as beautiful as a saint in a picture.
I wish I looked like her and walked the way she does. It's as
smooth as a swan swimming. I bounce too much. The sisters
said so and it's true. They said I laughed too much also.
I must try to be more stately.'

Maria tried being stately — for about five minutes. Curly
hair that slips out of whatever ribbons are twisted in it, eyes
that shine like an impish squirrel's, mouth that widens into
a friendly smile and makes a tipped-up nose crinkle — these
are all things that make being stately hard work. However,
Maria was doing her best as she came down the marble stairs

behind the Princess. The Princess was leaving. The stairs led out of the Coelhos' great hall into the entrance hall below.

Maria did not mean to smile when she saw Vasco. Only he looked so funny. His face was dirty and he had a black eye. His black hair stood on end and his plumed cap was on the back of his head. He had a coil of rope over one arm. The other was around a strange-looking brown-faced man with inky black hair and a torn robe that had once been white. It was stained now with mud and blood.

Vasco did not see the Princess at first. The light from the big wax candles was in his eyes. He spoke to the tall old Negro who had opened the big bronze doors. He looked like a bronze statue himself.

* Vasco said: 'Take Enrique, Fernan. He's hurt his foot and there's a cut on his arm. It's still bleeding a little. See what you can do for him. I will ask my father about sending him home.'

The big Negro said: 'Yes, Senhor Vasco. I will fix him up with some of that good African ointment of mine.'

He picked up Enrique as if the Malay were a small child and went off with him in his arms.

It was then that Vasco looked up and saw the Princess on the stairs above him. She had never looked more beautiful, he thought. Her ladies were around her, but, except for seeing Angela Luisa's red hair, he did not notice them. He heard Angela laugh and knew that someone else laughed at the same time.

The laughter made him remember that his clothes were torn and dirty. As usual when he saw the Princess, his feet and hands seemed much too big for him. He stumbled as he went towards the stairs in the flickering candlelight. The bow that was meant to be a graceful welcome to the Princess made him slip on the marble, and he found himself kneeling and looking down at her small velvet shoes.

He got to his feet somehow and began to stammer out that he was sorry to have been so clumsy.

It was then that Vasco looked up and saw the Princess on the stairs above him. She had never looked more beautiful, he thought.

'You're hurt,' the Princess said, in her soft voice that seemed like all the beautiful music that Vasco had ever heard.

'Only a few bruises,' he muttered awkwardly. 'They look worse than they are.'

'Tell me what happened, please,' Princess Isabella said.

When she spoke like that, slowly, but making her voice cool, like water running over marble, it was an order, Vasco knew. He made the story as short as he could. While he was telling it he saw the girl who was standing just behind the Princess at her left. He knew at once who it was who had been laughing at him. She was still smiling and she looked, Vasco thought, like a mischievous kitten. He wished suddenly that he had made himself out more of a hero.

His audience was getting larger. Christoval da Sousa and Shane O'Connor had been there from the first, escorting the ladies to the door, but Vasco had not noticed them. Now his father appeared and Vasco felt suddenly conscious of his father's quiet dignity and easy grace. There was a tall young man walking with Joan Coelho. He was taller than anyone there. Even Shane O'Connor had to look up at him. He was a fair-skinned, blue-eyed, rosy young man. With his glassy blue eyes and stiff curls the color of new butter he looked as highly colored as a painted wooden statue and — Vasco thought — as stupid.

He stood looking down at Vasco from his great height — the stairs gave him an extra foot — with his lip curved in a half-smile. The kind of smile a man might have for a beetle: if the beetle were on its back in the dust trying to turn over and if the man were going to step on it after a while.

'They ought to have him stuffed,' Vasco thought bitterly.

Then he felt better because his father was beside him and did not seem to notice that his son was battered and dirty or that he had come too late for the betrothal feast.

Vasco heard his father say, 'This is my son,' as if he were proud of him, as if Vasco were as neat and clean and prompt as Abraham, who was there too — looking pained.

The girl with the bush of brown curls was, Joan Coelho said, the niece of his old friend, Francisco da Sousa. That made Vasco look at her, because da Sousa was a great man. Senhor Magellan had said so.

The pink-faced popinjay with the butter-colored curls was called Juan Sebastian del Cano. Vasco had heard of him too. Christoval da Sousa had talked about him. Del Cano came from the Basque country and had commanded a ship for the King of Spain. He had saved da Sousa's life; rescued him from a shipwreck on the African coast with Moorish pirates attacking them. To da Sousa del Cano was a hero — Ulysses, Achilles, rolled into one. But Vasco still thought del Cano ought to be stuffed — or cast in bronze and stuck up in a public square somewhere.

When del Cano spoke to Vasco he did actually move — a little. He tipped his head back and dropped his eyelids with their pale lashes over his handsome blue eyes. It was his way of bowing apparently, and a great saving of motion, even if not especially courteous. He drawled out a few words in a voice that was fine and loud. It reminded Vasco of his own voice when he shouted into a wine barrel.

'I'm glad he is a stranger,' Vasco thought. 'The conceited oaf will sail away and I shall never have to see him again.'

Fortunately Vasco did not know at the moment just when del Cano would be sailing.

His father was speaking to him and Vasco forgot his dislike of del Cano.

'You had something you wished to give the Princess, I think,' he said. 'I sent for it.'

Vasco began to feel better. He saw one of the servants coming across the hall with the basket.

The Princess was sitting down now with her ladies around her. Joan Coelho had escorted her to a chair of carved oak and deep violet velvet. She looked even more beautiful in it than she had standing on the stairs. Her dress was pale violet. It was her favorite color, Vasco knew. She was like a violet in it, fresh and cool and sweet.

Vasco took the basket, looked into it for a moment, put a finger gently on something smooth and silky, and handed the basket to the Princess.

Long before Vasco was born — indeed before his godfather Vasco da Gama had reached India by sailing around Africa — there had come to Portugal a silky red Irish hunting dog named Connemara. He had come with Vasco's Irish uncle, Shane O'Connor. Later Shane had sent back to Ireland for a mate for Connemara. The red puppy sleeping in the basket was a great-great-grandson of Connemara's. His mother belonged to Vasco. There were six puppies in her latest family and the best one Vasco had chosen for the Princess, who had once admired the mother.

'He's ready to leave his mother now,' Vasco said. He forgot all about his hands and feet and about being embarrassed when the Princess thanked him and while he was telling her how to take care of the puppy.

The puppy stirred in his basket and put out his head.

'He has a beautiful face,' the Princess said. 'And his eyes — they are like topazes, and what lovely fringes on his ears! Oh, I must see him walk.'

She took the puppy out of the basket, held him against her cheek for a moment whispering something into his fringed ear, then set him down on the marble. The puppy's red paws spread in several directions at once and slid away from him. He lay there looking at the Princess adoringly, thumping his silky tail.

'You had better call him Vasco,' Angela Luisa said wickedly, and Vasco heard a giggle that he knew came from that girl with the bushy hair. Sebastian del Cano looked on with his bored half-smile. After a while he showed he was alive by yawning.

Vasco pretended he had not heard anyone laugh.

'He still drinks milk,' he said, picking up the puppy and putting him back in the basket, 'and he likes some raw beef finely chopped. No chicken bones — they splinter. A mutton bone is all right for him to use his teeth on.'

Getting the puppy back into the basket was about as easy as putting a shirt on a greased pig. There seemed to be much more puppy than there was basket. If Vasco got one leg in, three more came out. If all the legs were in, the puppy's head suddenly poked out, and of course there was always his feathery red tail to fan Vasco's hot face and tickle his wrists.

However, at last the puppy curled down, still turning a reproachful topaz eye up at Vasco. One of the servants who had come to escort the Princess back to the palace took the basket.

Vasco stood by his father as the stream of guests went past them. Sebastian del Cano, moving like a painted image carried on a cart; Christoval da Sousa, graceful and gay in white and gold; the Bishop in his violet robe with the cross of amethysts shining on his broad chest; ladies in wide skirts swishing over the marble like the waves lapping the sides of a boat; the troop of jugglers who had amused the guests — one of them was still tossing a scarlet ball; the musicians with their instruments wrapped up against the dampness of the river fog; dignified white-bearded men in long black robes; young men in doublets as bright as peacocks. Vasco grew dizzy with the river of color and sound. He knew that people looked at him with curiosity, that they would say to each other on the way home: 'Oh, yes — that was the other son — the queer one. Really he might have washed his face ... Now, Abraham is ——' all the excellent things that Abraham was, of course.

Vasco's head ached too much to care what they thought, or said. The Princess, when she thanked him for the puppy, had said to him softly: 'You saved that man's life. I know. You are a page to be proud of.'

So that girl with the gray-green eyes like a kitten could laugh at him all she liked ... And del Cano could look over his head with his conceited half-smile. What could Christoval see to admire in del Cano? Well, there must be something about him if Christoval liked him.

At last the hall was empty. The voices and the sound of the feet of horses and mules on the stones outside had died away. The candles, blown by the draft from the open doors, were dripping wax on the marble. Abraham began to put them out and the smell of the cooling wax filled the hall. The faint scent of violets that moved with the Princess was gone.

Vasco wondered if he could climb the stairs — this flight, then three more to his room at the top of the house. His legs seemed to be made of paper, and his feet of lead.

He started up the staircase yawning. Then he stopped, remembering the wounded Malay. He must see if he was all right.

He felt his father's arm around him.

'Enrique,' Vasco muttered. 'Find Enrique.'

'Fernan took him home,' Joan Coelho said quietly. 'Here is Fernan now, back again.'

The big Negro said: 'And just in time to carry Master Vasco to bed. Long time since I did that.'

Vasco felt himself being picked up. It felt wonderful not to have to move his feet. He was too tired to mind being carried. He was asleep before Fernan laid him on his bed, and slept on while the Negro and Joan Coelho undressed him.

They had to cut the sleeve away where it stuck to the deep gash on his arm.

'He must have lost much blood from that,' Joan Coelho said.

'Lucky his mother did not see that,' Fernan grunted. 'I wash it now, put some of my ointment on, that good African ointment of mine. I tie it up. We don't say anything to Senhora Coelho, because she is a lady that is timid about people being cut and bleeding.'

'You can't wash off that black eye,' Joan Coelho said. 'It shows worse than ever now his face is clean.'

'That is surely a fine black eye. I do not know if I ever saw one that was any worse looking. Still I will see what I can do with some of my good African ointment. You know that ointment of mine; it's good for cuts, bruises, burns, to rub on your chest if you have a bad cough . . .'

John Coelho laughed softly: 'Yes, I know, Fernan, and for smallpox and to make the girls admire you.'

'Senhor Vasco,' Fernan said, 'won't need it for that.'

THERE was always some mystery about why Vasco Coelho was dismissed by King Manuel. The King gave too many reasons. He was reorganizing his household, he said. He expected soon to marry a Spanish princess. (Marrying Manuel was a pleasure enjoyed by three Spanish princesses. One at a time, of course. The one he had in mind now, the third one, was a sister of the young King, Don Carlos the Fifth.)

His daughter, Manuel stated, would probably soon be married, too. Neither lady, he said, would need a page who came to Court looking like a professional wrestler. Pages were not supposed to be brawling in the streets at night. A few pages had been chosen to remain at Court. King Manuel said he was sorry that Vasco Coelho was not among them. His moradia would be paid until the end of the month, unless he left before. He was free to leave at any time.

And when he went, Manuel continued, he would kindly take with him the red dog with the extravagant appetite. With people starving in the world, Manuel did not, he said, approve of feeding a dog enough meat for a man. And milk! He himself never drank milk.

'No presents that eat while people starve,' King Manuel said, becoming really eloquent. 'This is a matter of principle with me.'

He did not say anything about how the puppy's milk and meat would be given to anyone who was starving.

Vasco, who was the only one of his family who was not angry with the King, decided that Manuel had dismissed him because the puppy ate too much. However, the red dog did not, after all, go home with him. Manuel had a soft spot in his heart and it was for the Princess. When she begged him to be allowed to keep the puppy, Manuel grumbled, but he gave in. The puppy was in her lap when Vasco said good-bye to her. He had decided to go at once and let the King save his milreis and barley.

'I am sorry you are going,' the Princess said, smoothing the puppy's shining head, 'but there must be something better for you to do than passing dishes, I think.'

'Generally upside down,' Vasco said with a smile.

The Princess smiled, too, and asked him what he was going to do.

'I should like to see if the world is round — but I suppose I'll stay in a warehouse and copy lists of spices.'

'The world *is* round, isn't it?'

'Yes, Your Highness, but there are many people who won't believe it until some one starts west and comes back from the east. Besides, I'd like to see what's down under our feet.'

'Tell me when you come back. I've heard it's dangerous — you have to walk with your head hanging down.' There was a gleam of mischief in Princess Isabella's soft blue eyes as she added: 'But perhaps it's no worse than walking through Lisbon at night. Thank you for the puppy. I was going to call him Apollo — he's so bright and beautiful — but I think after all his name will be Vasco.'

'Because he falls over his feet?' Vasco asked.

He heard Angela Luisa and the girl with the bush of brown curls giggling, but he didn't care.

'No,' said the Princess; 'because he wants to run and find out about everything, and because I know he's loyal and brave. Good-bye, Vasco. We will not forget you.'

'*Thank you for the puppy. I was going to call him Apollo — but I think, after all,
his name will be Vasco.*'

Vasco managed to get out of the room without falling over anything. He felt Maria da Sousa's eyes fixed on the back of his head as he went out the door.

'Let her laugh,' he thought, as he ran down the hill in the hot sunshine. He was glad to be out of the dim palace. He hated everything about it — giggling girls, stingy meals on splendid dishes, rules about how you stood and walked and bowed.

'In passing a dish to the Princess,' he could hear the school-master squeak, 'approach walking lightly, toes turned out, and step to her left. Your left foot is to be slightly advanced — thus. The left hand firmly spread under the dish; the right hand holding the napkin — don't crumple it as if it were a rag for cleaning a saddle — may be placed at your back, palm out, about half an inch above the hip bone. Stoop a little from the shoulders. Bend the right knee — no, Coelho — the *right* knee.'

Well, he'd never have to hear that again, Vasco thought. The only good thing about the Court was the Princess, and she would soon be gone: that is, if the new King of Spain had any sense. They said he was making up his mind whether to choose her or an English princess. A man in his senses would certainly choose Princess Isabella, Vasco decided. But, of course, Don Carlos had never seen her ...

Vasco's family were eating their dinner under the grape arbor. The grapes were beginning to get ripe. The sunshine brought out their fragrance. There were still a few roses — fragrant, too — and there was a fine rich smell of chicken cooked with paprika and of newly baked bread and of cakes spiced with cinnamon.

Senhor Magellan was sitting there quietly eating his dinner and Ruy Faleiro was talking fast and letting his paprika chicken and rice get cold on his plate.

Ruy Faleiro was angry about something — as usual. Old Zacuto looked as if he wished Faleiro would save his temper for time between meals.

'Anger is no sauce for food,' Grandfather Zacuto often said. 'If you wish to spoil your dinner, put red pepper on your own cake. Let others eat theirs in peace.'

This time Vasco was rather glad of Ruy Faleiro's bad temper. Faleiro was so enraged about Vasco's being dismissed by Manuel that no one else in the family had any chance to say anything. There was nothing for them to do but take it calmly while Faleiro paced up and down, snatching green grapes off the vine and throwing them around.

'I say this is spite, Magellan. It is aimed at you and me, because that spindle-shanked miser knows the boy has worked with us. I say we are in danger.' Here Faleiro absent-mindedly swallowed a green grape, and twisted his face into even angrier lines than usual. 'He is enraged because we have given up our citizenship. I told you we should not have done it so soon; it should have been kept secret till after we had gone. Now he begins persecuting us. What do you say to that, Magellan?'

Magellan, who was enjoying his stewed onions, said quietly that he doubted if King Manuel knew that Vasco had worked with them. As to giving up their citizenship, they had discussed that before.

'We agreed not to sneak out of the country, Faleiro. Besides, the King told me in public that I was free to offer my service anywhere I liked.'

'He said nothing of the sort to me,' Faleiro said. He had dropped into his seat and was messing the food about on his plate with a hunk of bread. 'The thing is aimed at me. He knows about my secret charts. Spies — there are spies everywhere.' He glared at Vasco. 'Did you tell anyone where the lantern's shadow fell? Magellan, we were fools to trust this boy.'

Shane O'Connor started up from the table at this, saying, 'Look here, my fine little astronomer!'

Joan Coelho flushed. Vasco saw his father's lips tighten as they did when he was angry.

Magellan said: 'You must forgive Faleiro. He is upset.'

Joan Coelho said, 'Senhor Faleiro is our guest, but I suggest that he forget this matter, and eat his dinner.'

There was something in Joan Coelho's quiet tones that silenced the astronomer for a moment. When he spoke again, it was more calmly.

'I should not have said that,' he said. 'I am sorry. The boy is a good boy — clever, too. But still there is something strange about his being dismissed from Court.'

'Nonsense,' said Shane O'Connor. 'Manuel was angry because Vasco gave the Princess a dog that would cost him something to feed. And it's true that he's cutting down his household. Let's think no more of it. The boy will come into the business with us. We can use someone who can read and write and speak French, and knock down thieves at night — can't we, Joan?'

'No doubt,' Joan Coelho said. 'Half a dozen if we had them.'

'That is all right for the boy,' Ruy Faleiro said stubbornly, 'but I still say, Magellan, that you and I are in danger. I think that attack last night was meant for me. It was at the time I often pass the Red Cat.'

'Perhaps it was,' Magellan said. 'Plenty of captains would like a good astronomer in their crews.'

'Well, then, what are you going to do about it?'

'I am going to Spain and — with his father's permission — I am going to take Vasco Coelho with me. I, too, can use a boy who can draw charts and knock down thieves, and who can take care of those who are supposed to protect him. That's what I came here today to say — when I found a chance to speak.'

Having spoken, Magellan went on eating.

After that everyone talked at once — everyone except Magellan and Vasco. Vasco did not hear what they said. He heard the blood beating loud in his ears, and felt his breath catch in his throat. He looked at Magellan to see if he really

meant it. Magellan looked back at Vasco, smiled in the way
that suddenly lighted his dark face, nodded without speaking,
then lifted his black eyebrows as if asking a question.

Vasco bowed his head quietly and the compact was made
between them. It was as if he had heard Magellan say, 'Will
you go with me?' And as if Vasco had answered, 'I will follow
you, Senhor, around the world, under it, to the end of it —
wherever you go.'

After a while he began to hear what they were all saying.
His grandfather said in a shaky voice, 'The boy seems very
young.' To Vasco's surprise it was his mother who answered.
He had expected her to try to make him stay at home. She
looked white, but she said quietly, 'I think he is not much
younger than his father was when he sailed around the Cape
of Storms.'

Abraham Zacuto squeaked: 'Now, that's true. You're a
very remarkable girl, Rachel. Isn't she, Joan?'

Joan Coelho picked up his wife's hand and kissed it. 'She
always was,' he said.

'No,' said Rachel Coelho. 'It's only that I know that young
ducks have to swim. I've always known Vasco would go to
sea sometime. If he is to sail with anyone, I am glad to think
it will be with Senhor Magellan.'

'I thank you for that, Senhora,' Magellan said, 'but for a
time our sailing will be on dry land — to Spain.'

'And it had better be soon,' Ruy Faleiro muttered, 'and the
less talk about it the better.'

Much to Vasco's relief, Ruy Faleiro did not go with them
when they set out for Seville. Just why Faleiro decided to
stay in Lisbon, Magellan never said. Perhaps Faleiro expected by talking to seamen in Lisbon taverns to find out
more about the route they must follow to reach the Spice
Islands by sailing west. Perhaps his black temper had burst
out again and had been followed by one of those fits of gloom
in which he would speak to no one. He may still have been
afraid of spies and have thought that it would deceive the

spies if Magellan started alone. Whatever the reason was, Faleiro was not one of the party that left Lisbon that cool September morning. Magellan was not the only captain leaving Manuel's service. There were several dissatisfied pilots leaving Portugal to seek their fortune in Spain.

It was still dark when Vasco got on his mule for the journey, but the courtyard was crowded with the family and servants of the great house. Afterwards Vasco remembered his mother, pale but smiling, his Uncle Shane's red beard flashing in the lantern light, Abraham's neat clothes and peevish voice, his father's hand on his shoulder and his quiet 'Fair winds, Vasco.'

His Aunt Luisa said, 'I wish I were going,' and his uncle laughed and called: 'Hurry away, boy, before she gets on a mule and races you to Spain. If it was a ship, now, she'd stow away on it.'

In a moment the gate shut behind them and the voices calling good wishes were shut behind the wall. The mule bells began to tinkle as they followed the road up the hill. The houses above them were still inky black against a sky that was beginning to change from greenish silver to pale gold. A star as bright as a blazing candle was slipping down behind the dark mass of the palace. In the midst of that jumble of courts, walls, roofs, and balconies was the room where the Princess was sleeping. Beyond it was a row of small rooms where the ladies-in-waiting slept. The rooms were like cells in a convent, Angela had said, only colder. Manuel did not approve of tapestries and stamped leather to keep drafts off ladies-in-waiting, or of charcoal braziers where they could warm their cold fingers.

'Keep warm with your work,' was Manuel's advice.

Vasco wished he had seen Angela Luisa again. She had teased him and laughed at him, but now that he was going away he realized that she had always been more fun than his own sisters — more like a brother than Abraham, who never had time to run races and climb trees and fall off horses, or

put toads in his bed. He wondered if she knew he was going
that morning. It was her turn to sleep at the palace that
week, and she had not been at home for several days.

'I ought to have sent her a message,' he thought.

Now the star had gone and the palace was turning from
black to misty gray. They were passing the gate of the courtyard where Vasco had once been pitched into a rosebush. It
seemed a long time ago. The gate was open a little way.
Someone had been careless, Vasco thought.

Then his mule shied and almost threw him off. Two dark
figures were slipping out of the clump of evergreens near the
gate. When Vasco had stopped the mule and straightened
himself in the saddle, he found himself looking down into
Angela Luisa's face. Maria da Sousa was just behind her.
They looked as pleased as kittens that have eaten a dish of
sardines.

'What are you doing here?' Vasco asked. The words
seemed to be jolted out of his mouth.

'Spoken like a true courtier,' Angela said. 'Wouldn't you
know he had been educated at King Manuel's Court, Maria?
In answer to your polite question, Senhor Vasco Coelho, I will
tell you that we have been shivering in those prickly bushes
for half an hour, listening for mule bells. That we borrowed
a key. That if King Manuel finds out, he will shut us up on
bread and water — or anyway water — for a week.'

Maria laughed. She had a rather pretty laugh, but Vasco
only scowled at her.

'We came,' Angela Luisa went on, 'to say good-bye to
Senhor Magellan. Maria knows him.'

'I saw him at my uncle's house when I was — when I was
younger than I am now. He risked his life to save me from
terrible danger.'

She had put on a grave expression, but was having trouble
with her dimples.

'You'd better go in,' Vasco said severely. 'My master has
no time to waste.'

Just then Magellan rode around the corner of the wall. It was getting light now and Vasco could see that Magellan was smiling. The way he could tell was by the creases at the corners of his master's eyes. His heavy black beard and his mustache hid his mouth.

'I was afraid you had been attacked by robbers, Coelho,' he said.

'It's only my cousin, Senhor, and her friend, Dona Maria da Sousa,' Vasco said hastily.

Angela Luisa said, 'I said he had courtly manners. "Only my cousin and her friend." What a graceful way of presenting us to you, Senhor, when we came out before dawn to see you!'

The creases deepened around Magellan's eyes as he said: 'It was very kind of you ladies to come out so early to see — me. Did you say da Sousa was your friend's name?'

'You knew my Uncle Francisco da Sousa, Senhor Magellan, and you saved my life once,' Maria da Sousa said.

Magellan really smiled this time. 'Were you the baby in the cradle? The one I carried out when Don Francisco's house caught fire?'

'Yes, and a bronze bust of Cicero under the other arm, and a cage with a parrot hung around your neck, I've always heard. I thought it was time I thanked you, Senhor.'

'You are welcome, Dona Maria. It was only a small fire. There was really no danger — they soon put it out; but how that parrot cursed in good Portuguese, and how you howled!'

Vasco laughed at this account of the romantic way in which Maria's life had been saved. He received an indignant look from the heroine of the adventure.

Mules were still being driven past them. To protect themselves from possible attack by robbers they had joined a party bound for Seville and there was a long line of pack mules carrying merchandise. Their own baggage appeared, and Magellan said good-bye to the two girls and moved off.

'I must go,' Vasco said.

'We brought you something,' Angela Luisa said.

She pushed a small bundle into the pocket of his saddle-bags. 'Come back and tell us what it's like around the world.'

'What shall I bring you?'

'Oh, a baby tiger or a pet snake with jewelled eyes, or a seed from the tree that drops pearls into oysters.'

'And would you like something?' Vasco asked Maria. 'Something easy, please. A young elephant. Or a magic carpet that flies in the air. Or a feather from the tail of the bird that turns everything to gold — whatever you like.'

'You don't need to bring anything,' Maria da Sousa said, 'only ——'

'Only what?'

'Good-bye,' Maria said, and the two girls disappeared into the shadowy courtyard. Before he could say anything — even if he had thought of anything to say — a door clanged behind them.

The silk wrappings of whatever it was that Angela had stuffed into his saddlebag caught his eye. He drew it out and opened it. There was a letter on top in Angela's writing.

Dear Vasco [it said]:

Maria and I saved all our sweets this week and got the cook to make you some honey cakes. They have dates and nuts in them. Of course now we are starving, but it doesn't matter what happens to girls. I wish I were a boy and could go with you. Instead I am going to be a great artist. I have been taking lessons for three weeks. My teacher says I have great natural talent. Probably I get it from Uncle Dennis. You know that portrait of Vasco da Gama he painted that hangs in the great hall? The one that used to frighten me till I cried? My teacher says I have the same gift Uncle Dennis had for catching a likeness. The locket has my two best pictures that I have painted so far in it. When you get home I will do one of you.

The other Vasco is well. He is learning to follow when
the Princess tells him to.

Good-bye, Vasco, from your cousin, the famous painter.

Angela Luisa Coelho O'Connor.

Vasco unwrapped the locket. It was of gold set with
pearls. He remembered seeing Angela wear it, but the cord
was new. It was made of twisted gold thread with small
pearls knotted into it every few inches. He opened the case.
Yes, it was true. Angela had a gift for getting a likeness.
There was the Princess in her dress of pale violet, looking as
she had that night of the betrothal feast. In the other side
of the locket was Maria da Sousa's impish face, dimples,
gray-green eyes, curly bush of hair. Angela had left out the
freckles, but even without them it was hard on Maria to be
put into a locket next to the Princess.

It would be hard on anyone, Vasco decided kindly. He shut
the locket, put the cord around his neck, shoved one of the
honey cakes into his mouth and the rest into the saddlebag,
and began to fold up the letter. There was a sentence at the
end that he had missed. It said: 'Maria made the cord. She
thinks you're wonderful.'

After all, Vasco thought, as he rode along at the end of
the mule train, Maria da Sousa was not a bad-looking girl —
if she did have freckles — if you didn't always see her with the
Princess.

He wondered what she had started to say to him. Then he
forgot all about her.

The sun was coming up now over Spain. Vasco rode towards it, sometimes eating honey cakes, sometimes singing.

4039

LONG DAYS WAITING ———————————— 6

WHEN Vasco rode off towards Spain that morning, it never occurred to him that he would be there for two years. He never thought that in those years he and his master would meet disappointment and treachery or that Manuel's spite would follow Magellan into Spain. Luckily Spain was ruled by a man as different from Manuel as a lion is from a hyena.

At least that is what Vasco thought, and he knew both Kings. He was at Valladolid in 1517 when Don Carlos the Fifth, grandson of Ferdinand and Isabella, was crowned there. Magellan had sent Vasco ahead from Seville to get lodgings ready. Soon after Magellan arrived in Seville he was betrothed to Beatriz Barbosa, daughter of an old friend, Diego Barbosa. Diego, a distant cousin of Magellan's, had come to Spain because he, too, had tired of King Manuel's service. Magellan planned that after his wedding and as soon as the officials of India House in Seville decided to recommend his voyage to the Spice Islands to the King, then he and his young wife would journey to Valladolid. Faleiro had arrived in Seville and would travel with them, Magellan wrote to Vasco. It would not be long now, he said.

It was longer than he thought. The men at India House at first looked coldly on Magellan's scheme for reaching the

Spice Islands by sailing west. Faleiro's explosions of temper caused delays. When he arrived at Seville, he was furious because Magellan had admitted to Juan Aranda, the most friendly of the India House officials, that Magellan and Faleiro planned to go from the Atlantic to the Pacific by a strait that led from one ocean to the other.

Faleiro said Magellan had betrayed them. He would not believe that Aranda was enough of a geographer to have guessed that if Magellan and Faleiro planned to sail to the Spice Islands in Spanish waters, as Magellan had said, they must either sail around the tip of South America or find a strait farther north. They could not follow the Portuguese route east around the Cape of Good Hope; King Manuel's captains would never allow that, Aranda knew. If they went west, they must either sail around South America or find a passage across it somewhere. The Spaniards had already thought of digging a canal across the Isthmus of Panama, but had given up the task. It was impossible, they decided. However, there might be a passage somewhere south of Brazil and far enough west to be in Spanish territory.

The line that divided the world into two halves — one Spanish and one Portuguese — ran west of Brazil. Magellan and Faleiro had a map showing how the South American coast sloped away to the west and became Spanish ground. In Lisbon they had seen a map, drawn by an old Portuguese pilot, with a strait leading into the Pacific marked on it. They had not drawn the strait on their own map, but Aranda had guessed it.

Magellan's days in Seville went by in quarrels with Faleiro, in bargaining with Aranda, who wanted part of the profits of the voyage if he interested the King and his ministers in it, in preparations for his wedding, in explaining geography to the officers at India House. India House was so named because it was in command of the affairs of the West Indies. Its officials sent ships to the new world, which Columbus had discovered, and watched for them to come back laden with gold. These men knew about every crumb of biscuit and every dried fig eaten by the sailors sent to the Indies. They knew just how much sailcloth and how many casks of wine were needed for a three months' voyage. Yet somehow they failed to see in the black-bearded, brown-faced man with the lame knee the greatest navigator they would ever know.

They thought his scheme crazy. Reach the Spice Islands by sailing west? Nonsense! And suppose he did — how about the Portuguese? They'd let him do it quietly, would they? A likely story.

So they ate a hearty dinner and had a good sleep about it, thinking they had disposed forever of the lame Portuguese sailor and his wild ideas.

In Seville Faleiro sulked. Aranda said he would like a fifth of the profits of the voyage — but would take an eighth. Vasco, waiting in Valladolid, found the days long. Magellan had given him money, but as the days stretched into weeks, the money began to run out. Fortunately the innkeeper was good-natured and Vasco made himself useful. He groomed horses, fed mules, carried water, shelled chestnuts, washed dishes, sang to the innkeeper's little boy. Vasco's voice was changing, but Tonio did not mind if Vasco sang like a thrush one minute and a crow the next. He liked it. He was a little fat boy. You could see just how he would look when he became a large fat innkeeper. He was always at Vasco's heels. He would trot into the stable where Vasco was feeding mules and grooming horses.

'Sing me the song about "The world is round." Sing about "Down under,"' he would say.

Vasco, who was always glad of some company besides that of horses, would croak out the song. He had made up the words and the tune that went with them himself. It wasn't much of a tune, but singing it made him feel that he would not have to spend all his life in a stable.

When he sang, the noise of horses drinking became the sound of water against a ship's side. The old beams of the

'Sing me the song about "The world is round." Sing about "Down under,"'
he would say.

stable were the ship's timbers, newly washed shirts flapping
outside in the breeze were sails in the wind . . .

> 'I will see if the world is round.
> I will sail where they make the thunder.
> I will walk on the spicy ground
> Down under.'

Here Vasco would begin brushing the dust out of a mule's
mouse-colored coat. 'Look out for his heels, Tonio. Sit over
there on the bucket.'

'Yes. Sing some more.'

> 'I will see the moon to bed
> And the waves foam up above her.
> I will watch where the sun shines red
> Up over . . .'

'Hand me that brush, Tonio . . . S-sh, mule . . . S-sh . . .
Stand over!' he would say, and Tonio would order, 'Sing some
more.'

> 'We will seek no peace nor rest
> Till the stars and winds give warning
> That where East turns to West
> Night's morning.'

'Sing some more!'

'There isn't any more — not till I make up some.'

'Tell about Tonio the Fish, then.'

Tonio the Fish was a fish who had adventures — a new one
every day. He was swallowed by a whale. He rode on a dolphin's back, grew wings, learned to fly. He ate a diamond and
found it did not agree with him. He got tangled up in a mer-
maid's hair. He was always in trouble and was always getting
out again as he swam gaily around the world.

One morning Vasco heard a splash. It seemed to come from
a pool back of the stable where a hurrying brook had made a
bowl for itself. He ran towards the pool. There was something red in it, bright red, the color of Tonio's jerkin. Vasco
got to the pool just in time to pull out a well-soaked, shivering,
sputtering Tonio.

'I was a fish with wings. I was swimming,' Tonio stated between coughs and gasps.

'You were swimming like a stone,' Vasco said, 'and if you try it again, I won't tell you any more stories.'

Tonio gave up being a fish. Tonio's mother hugged Vasco and kissed him and cried down his neck. Vasco wiggled away only to find himself being slapped on the back and kissed on both cheeks by the innkeeper. Vasco began to think better of horses. After all, they never kissed him. From that day Tonio's mother always cooked him special dishes and embarrassed him very much by telling everyone who came to the inn that he was the savior of her child.

Still there were pleasant things about the inn. On cold evenings they would sit around the fire and toast chestnuts. You cut across on the humped side of the chestnuts and put them near the hot coals. If you didn't cut them, they went off with a bang and shot out into the room, scattering ashes about. After a while Tonio would fall asleep and his mother would pick him up and put him in a bed that was a box along the wall.

Vasco would sit for a while in the firelight writing letters home. One night in November he wrote to his mother:

'Today has been a great day in Valladolid. Don Carlos came here to be crowned. We were out on the street for a long time watching for him to come, Tonio and I. We were lucky to find a wall to climb. That is, I climbed. First I pushed Tonio up. We sat up there in the sunshine eating nuts and raisins. After there were prickles in my feet because they were hanging down so long, we saw something shining a long way off and we heard drums and trumpets and people shouting. In a few minutes they came past the corner of the wall and we could look down on the heads of marching men and into the faces of the horsemen.

'First there were thirty falconers with their birds on their wrists, the birds all hooded in bright silk and their bells tinkling. There were men with halberds, men with lances, men

pounding drums and blowing fifes. The King's horses, all
with trappings of velvet and gold, were led by their grooms.
Even the grooms were better dressed than King Manuel.
The great nobles from Flanders and Spain were there, and
ambassadors and heralds. I never saw so many flags. And I
think there must have been a thousand men in the procession.

'The King rode his horse as if it were part of him. He wore
steel armor with a coat of crimson silk and a cloak of gold and
silver brocade over it. The ostrich plumes on his black velvet
cap came so close to us that I could see how they were fas-
tened on with a buckle of pearls and rubies. Tonio tried to
grab for them and we almost fell off the wall, and then he
yelled, "Long live our King Don Carlos" so loud that the
King turned and smiled up at him. He has big dark blue
eyes, chestnut hair, a long chin that sticks out, and a high
forehead. They call him the Boy King, but he looks like a
man and a sensible one. He is fine looking when he smiles.

'When he had passed, we jumped down and ran by back
streets and squeezed in near the door of the cathedral. I
took Tonio on my shoulders. I thought he would break my
neck. We could not see much except the banners. There was
one for each place where the King rules. There were so many
that the church seemed hung with bright silks and gold. We
could hear them call out his titles and when they called a name
a banner would be lowered. They began, "Carlos, by the
grace of God, Archduke of Austria, Prince of Burgundy,
Count of Flanders." I can't remember half of them but they
ended with "Lord of the Americas," and then I suppose the
Cardinal must have put the crown on his head, because the
banners all rose again and the gray place was all floating color.

'They say he will be the Holy Roman Emperor too. And
when we come back from our voyage he will be lord of countries no one has ever heard of. Yet he is kind and simple. He
looks grave, but he can joke. You know how it is when a king
makes a joke. Everyone laughs, but the laughter sounds thin
and hollow. When Don Carlos came out of the church he

said something that made the men around him really laugh — not just pretend to laugh. I did not hear what he said, of course, but afterwards I heard one of the men who is staying at our inn tell about it.

'Someone showed the King a monument in the square and read him the words carved on it, "Here lies a man who never knew fear."

'"Oh," said the King, "then he can never have put out a candle with his fingers."

'I like that. I keep thinking about it. I suppose he meant that no one is really brave who hasn't been afraid and fought against his fear and won. If you are afraid to pinch out a candle flame but do it just the same, then you know something about courage. And only a really brave man would admit that he understood little fears.

'Do you remember that Sebastian del Cano, the one like the wooden image? He is here. He had dinner at our inn the day they were telling what the King said. I waited on him. Of course he did not know me. He is the sort of man that never looks at the servants. You run back and forth, pouring wine, bringing water for his hands, slicing hot roast pork off the loin on the spit, and cracking walnuts for him, and then he looks somewhere past your left ear and says: "Oh — are you our waiter? Well, bring me ——" whatever he wants, probably something we haven't got.

'When they told what the King had said about snuffing candles, del Cano put down a pork chop he was gnawing and gave a kind of snort, "They say he's afraid of spiders too," he said. "A pity our new King's a coward!"

'One of the others took offense at that, but his friends held him down. Del Cano only laughed when the man came at him with his dagger. He picked up his chop and finished it. When he got ready he threw the bone to a beggar at the door and swaggered off. I suppose he's brave too — the other kind of brave man, the kind without imagination. Probably there'll be a statue of him sometime with fine words on it. They say

he is going to ask the King for the command of a galleon. I
hope he will get it and sail a long way off.'

This letter was many weeks reaching Portugal. By the
time it was being read aloud around the Coelhos' fire, Magellan
had arrived in Valladolid.

VASCO had no time to play with Tonio now. Faleiro and Aranda had come as well as Magellan and his wife. Vasco was kept busy waiting on them all. Faleiro was in one of his sulky moods. He refused to speak to Aranda, but he did not object to Aranda's paying for his dinner. 'He is going to make a fortune out of us — let him pay,' he grumbled.

Faleiro was angry because Magellan had agreed to give Aranda an eighth of whatever profits came from the voyage. Aranda would never really help them with the King, Faleiro said. He was a cheat and a thief.

Aranda, however, did help them to an audience with the King. It was only a few days after Magellan's party arrived in Valladolid that Magellan and Faleiro were presented to the King.

Vasco wrote about it to his father.

'Today we went to the palace at the time Don Carlos was dining. Juan Aranda, of whom I have written before, went with us to introduce Senhor Magellan and Ruy Faleiro to the King. Bishop Fonseca was there, also a cardinal from the Low Countries — a pleasant man but one who does not know much about geography, I think. The Bishop knows a good deal. He learned it because he said Christopher Columbus would never find anything by sailing west. Now he does not think the world is flat any longer. So that is something. He seemed interested in our voyage and if he helps us, then I will say he is the best geographer in the world. We went past the house today where Columbus died. He was poor and alone.

'"That is all you get from princes," Faleiro said, "a chance to die alone in a dirty cold room after you discover a new world for them."

'Juan Aranda said that Ferdinand Columbus, the explorer's son, was a great nobleman and very rich from his father's discoveries. Faleiro said that did not do his father much good. Senhor Magellan did not say anything for a while, but at last he spoke. He never talks loud, but he can always make Ruy Faleiro be silent. "Columbus opened a new world. He saw what was there. That was enough for him."

'"It wouldn't be enough for me," Faleiro muttered, but so low that Magellan did not hear it. Soon we were in the dining hall of the palace and he kept quiet.

'The room is a very fine one, hung with new tapestries brought from Flanders by the King. They have special skill there in this work, it seems. The ones we saw that day told the story of the Trojan War. I never saw tapestry with colors so rich or so finely blended.

'The King sat alone at a table between the windows. There were eight pages serving. The dinner was of four courses. The pages place the dishes on the table and draw off the silver covers. If the King does not care for what is on the dish, he shakes his head and the page carries the dish away. If the King is suited, he bows his head and pulls the dish towards him.

'There were great pies of game, a big joint of roast beef, and a calf's head, besides bread and sweets. No one carved for him. He cut himself a piece of game pie and sliced off some of the calf's head. He did not put his knife in his mouth as King Manuel does. He began by cutting up bread into pieces big enough for a mouthful and then covering them with meat and gravy. He used his fingers for the bread and held his plate under his chin with his other hand. He ate so neatly that we all took pleasure in watching him.

'There were two silver flagons of wine on the sideboard and a crystal goblet. He had it filled three times by the butler, who looked as grave as a doctor of medicine. The King would empty it all each time at one drink. He took no notice of the crowd that was watching him. His buffoon, a fat, humped little dwarf, was there, and did all kinds of tricks to entertain his master. The King did not seem much amused, though once in a while he gave a sort of half-smile.

'Then the pages carried away the table and the sideboard and moved the King's chair near one of the windows. He sat there in the sunshine and anyone could go up and speak to him or hand him a paper with a petition written on it. His chair was of crimson velvet with gold fringe. He was plainly dressed in fine black cloth, with no ornaments except a jewel hung around his neck by a gold cord.

'At last it was Senhor Magellan's turn to go up to the King. I walked behind him carrying the globe and the charts. Faleiro slunk along cracking his fingers and staring at everything — you know how he does. Juan Aranda is a tall man — as tall as I am — fine looking with a big smooth voice. Faleiro looks wild, but he is handsome in that strange way that you remember. You remember, too, that my master is little and shabby and how he limps. Yet it was at him the King looked and to him that he listened. The Bishop was there beside him.

'After a while the King called the Cardinal over to him, too. Don Carlos does not speak Portuguese and only a few words of Spanish, so the talk was all in French. I understood pretty well. I was glad for the words they beat into me at Court. The Bishop told him in French what Senhor Magellan and Faleiro and Juan Aranda said. I spun the globe for them and Faleiro showed them how the Spice Islands may well lie in Spanish waters. Then I unrolled the charts and Senhor Magellan showed how he would sail and told how he was sure there was a strait through from the Atlantic to the Pacific, but that if he did not find it, then he would sail south around the end of South America, because no doubt it ended in a cape just as Africa does at the Cape of Good Hope.

'The King said nothing all this time, only nodded once in a while to show he understood. When Senhor Magellan finished speaking, he said: "Thank you, Senhor. I will think of what you have said."

'Then Senhor Magellan and Faleiro and Aranda made their bows and moved off, but I was still rolling up the maps. Then I heard the King say in Franch, "Please let me look at that map again."

'It was the one showing the strait and I unrolled it for him and held it while he sat looking at it a while, not saying anything.

'At last he thanked me. He has a way of speaking so that you forget you are a page and he is a king. He seems to forget it himself. He said, "Would you like to sail into these places that may not even be there at all?"

'I said, "Your Majesty, I would follow my master around the world and home again even if the ships sailed upside down and backwards all the way."

'He smiled at that and took the map, looked closely at it for a minute, then rolled it up neatly and handed it back to me. "I thought he was that sort of man," he said.

'Then he made a sign with his hand, something the way King Manuel does, only when Don Carlos does it there's something grand about it — kind, too. I bowed as well as I could with the maps under my arm and the globe in my hands and moved out of the way of someone coming up behind me. It was Sebastian del Cano. He almost knocked the globe out of my hands with his elbow. He had his hand on his sword hilt, of course, and he was stuffed into a light blue velvet suit with silver on it. When I left the hall he was telling the King all about Juan Sebastian del Cano. It seems he's wonderful. You could hear him out on the stairs. . . . Well, Christoval says he is a fine navigator. Perhaps he is not so stupid as he seems.

'I ran all the way back to the inn. It is frosty and nipping here now. Faleiro drank too much at supper and talked too loud about sailing around the world. This was after Senhor Magellan had gone to bed or it would not have happened. One of the men listening to Faleiro and buying wine for him was a man named Alvarez. I saw him once at King Manuel's Court and I would not trust him any farther than I would a rat with a hunk of cheese. He is an agent of King Manuel's, I think.'

Vasco wrote another letter — a short one — to Angela Luisa. In it he said: 'You will hear all about what we have been doing from my other letters, but I wanted to tell you about the locket. I was kneeling down rolling up some maps and the King asked me for one back and after he had looked at it and asked me some questions, he said: "Your locket is unfastened. It would be a pity if you lost the pictures out of it. Your sisters' pictures, I suppose."

'"No, Sire," I said. "I was a page to one of the ladies in Portugal and the other is one of her ladies-in-waiting. My cousin is one too. She painted them."

'"Whose page were you?" he asked, and I told him Dona Isabella's.

'"My little cousin," he said, and looked at the picture for a while. He didn't say anything about it except that the pictures were neatly painted, but I think he liked it. Only they say now he is going to marry a French princess. I hope it is not true.'

Vasco did not say why he hoped Don Carlos was not going to marry a French princess.

Angela Luisa, reading the letter in Portugal weeks later, said that it was exactly like Vasco to leave out just what you wanted to hear.

'I think he writes wonderful letters,' Maria da Sousa said. 'Most boys can't write at all, and the ones who can just sit and tickle their ears with the feather and then say: "I have been too busy to write. I am well. My dog is well. I hope you are well, too. We had roast pig for dinner. This quill is no good, so excuse the blots. I must go to my riding lesson now, so goodbye."'

'Well, I suppose Vasco's letters are a little better than that,' Angela Luisa said. 'Anyway, I hope he'll write again soon.'

ON THE twenty-second of March, 1518, Magellan, Faleiro, and Aranda were still in Valladolid — waiting. They had finished dinner and now were sitting around a half-dead fire. There was a cold wind blowing outside. It set dust clouds whirling over everything.

Beatriz Barbosa Magellan was working on a piece of embroidery. Ruy Faleiro dozed in his chair with his feet stuck out towards the fire. Enrique went about his business of clearing the table. He shivered as the wind blew loud in the chimney and puffed ashes over the floor. Magellan and Aranda had shoved the dishes away from their end of the table and had papers spread out in front of them. Aranda was checking over lists of figures. Magellan was studying a chart.

The room was quiet. The sounds in it were all so small that they could not be heard except when the wind stopped its blustering for a moment. Then you could hear the scratching of Aranda's quill, the padding of Enrique's soft-shod feet, Faleiro's breathing, an occasional snap from the half-burned chestnut logs.

Enrique dropped a pewter dish. It hit another and the clang made the astronomer stop dozing. He got out of his chair, cursed Enrique for waking him, and strode over to the window. For a minute he stared at the whirling dust clouds. Then he began to pace up and down and bite his nails. He did not speak and no one spoke to him. Now and then he glared at Magellan out of his strange yellow-brown eyes. Once he paused and looked down at the chart, but after a moment he shrugged his narrow shoulders and went back to the window, muttering something.

Beatriz Magellan, a small, fair woman, who looked gentle, patient, and ill, kept her eyes on her work. Faleiro frightened her. Sometimes she thought she could not bear another meal with him while he raged at Aranda and Magellan. This sulky silence was better, but when he began to make that purring growl in his throat, she knew that he would soon lash out again.

Magellan paid no attention to the astronomer. To him Faleiro was no more annoying than thunder, wind, hail, dust, or rain. You just let them sweep over you and thought of something else. After a while the sun would come out. Faleiro was tiresome, but he was clever. He had a scheme for measuring longitude that Magellan felt sure would tell accurately the place of a ship on the earth's surface. Neither Columbus nor da Gama had been able to be sure how far east or west a ship had travelled. With Faleiro's tables of longitude ... Faleiro stopped near the table and said, 'What chart is that?'

'A copy of one used by the great Admiral Christopher Columbus on his last voyage,' Magellan said.

Faleiro said scornfully: 'He didn't know where he was going. When he got there he didn't know where he was, and when he got home he didn't know where he'd been.'

'He was the greatest navigator the world has ever seen,' Magellan said quietly.

'But he'd have been greater still if he'd had Faleiro with him.'

Faleiro made this modest statement and swaggered over to the fire and kicked the smouldering logs so that one broke with a crunch and yellow flames began to lick around the pieces.

Outside the wind was still howling. It blew so hard that it sounded to Beatriz Magellan like horses galloping. Then the wind dropped and the galloping went on. It stopped and there was a knock at the door, a loud, confident knock; then there were voices and feet stumbling upstairs.

Vasco, out of breath, his hair on end, dashed into the room stammering, 'Senhor Magellan, the courier, the courier from the King.'

The courier followed him more sedately. He was a fat red-faced man with his fine clothes dusty from his ride.

'To Ferdinand Magellan, Knight, and to Ruy Faleiro, Bachelor, from our most noble King Don Carlos,' he said, handed a sealed packet to Magellan, made a magnificent sweeping bow, and began to warm his back at the fire, adding, 'Dry work riding today.'

'Vasco, some wine for His Majesty's courier,' Magellan said, so Vasco had to miss seeing the packet opened. The paper was spread out on the table when he came back with the wine. Faleiro was reading it aloud over Magellan's shoulder in a voice cracking with excitement. As Vasco moved around filling wine cups he learned that Don Carlos gave Magellan and Faleiro permission to explore in the Pacific, that they must keep out of Portuguese lands and water, that they should have a share of all profits of the voyage and be made governors of all lands they might discover. Their titles were to be borne by their heirs forever. If they found more than six islands, they might choose two of any extra ones they found for themselves and have part of the revenue from them forever. The King promised to equip five ships, and pay crews of two hundred and thirty-four men. He would provide artillery and food for two years. Magellan was to have power of life and death over all officers and men by land or sea. He and Faleiro were to be captains general. Magellan — instead of his Portuguese title of nobility, which he had given up with his Portuguese citizenship — was to be a Knight of the Order of Saint James, and Faleiro was made a Knight, too. He swaggered more than ever at this and snapped his fingers. 'Sir Ruy Faleiro. Sir Ruy Faleiro,' he muttered to himself. 'It sounds well, very well.'

No one but Vasco heard him because Aranda was talking loud and congratulating Magellan and slapping the courier on the back and pouring out wine. Beatriz Magellan had tears rolling down her cheeks and falling on her embroidery. She wiped her eyes with the embroidery so that her husband would not see the tears, and said, 'Ferdinand, you must have a new cloak now, and a new suit to wear to Court when the King knights you.'

Magellan smiled at her and said gently, 'Why, I will wear my wedding suit to Court, and I have a very good cloak — not five years old,' and went back to his papers. He was the least excited of anyone in the room. Even the King's courier began to talk about sailing around the world.

Magellan read quietly through the long contract. It began: 'I, Don Carlos, by the grace of God, King of Castille, Leon, Aragon, and the two Sicilies, of Jerusalem, and of Navarre, Granada, Toledo, Valencia, Galicia, the Mallorcas, Sardinia, Cordova, the Algarves, Gibraltar, of the Canary Isles, of the Indies, isles and mainland of the Ocean Sea, Count of Barcelona, Lord of Biscay, Duke of Athens, Count of Roussillon, Marquis of Luristan, Archduke of Austria, Duke of Brabant, Count of Flanders and Tyrol . . .'

At the end of it was the King's signature — Yo el Rey — I, the King.

There was a copy of the agreement for Magellan and Faleiro to sign. Magellan wrote his name — he used the Spanish form of it, Vasco noticed — steadily and carefully. Faleiro added his trembling scrawl. The courier looked carefully in the wine jug, saw that it was empty, took the paper to carry to the King, and went out into the wind and dust.

Faleiro was wildly gay that night. He sang. He talked about islands full of gold and pearls and strange fruits, of birds with jewelled feathers, of trees that rained rubies. 'You shall have a feather cloak, Senhora,' he said to Beatriz, 'so thin it will go through a bracelet, yet each feather is of gold. Diamonds will shine in your hair. A thousand slaves shall do your bidding. They will scatter strange perfumes before you and flowers will grow wherever you walk. After we find six islands — only six islands — your husband and I can each choose one.

'We will sail about in the sunshine choosing them. There we will build palaces of spicy woods. The very rafters will smell of cinnamon. I shall be rowed over to see you in a boat built out of nutmeg wood and sheathed with gold. Twenty rowers I'll have, slaves of mine, and every one with pearls as big as chestnuts in his ears. I'll sit under an awning of gold tissue fringed with emeralds ——'

There was a great deal more of this, but Beatriz Magellan did not seem to be listening to him. She watched her husband's quiet shabby figure as he limped to the fire and stood looking into it. 'I wish you would not go, Ferdinand,' she murmured, during one of Faleiro's loud bursts of singing. 'I am afraid for you.'

'It's hard to stay at home and be brave — but you'll do it for me,' Magellan said gently.

Never again, Vasco remembered afterwards, did she show her fear. For the rest of the time before they sailed — all those long months still to come — she was cheerful.

As for Faleiro, he soon sank back into gloom and sulks. On the whole Vasco preferred him when he was gloomy. It was easier to work when Faleiro was quiet, and there was much work in equipping five ships to sail around the world.

OF KING MANUEL'S spies in Spain, Sebastian Alvarez was the cleverest. He was in charge of Portuguese goods sent to Spain, but he found time for other things. Alvarez was not above listening at keyholes or bribing servants to tell tales about their masters. He was very good at opening letters and fastening them up again so that the seal looked as good as new.

Trying to bribe Vasco to open Magellan's letters, however, was a mistake. Alvarez began by congratulating Vasco on the fine contract his master had signed with Don Carlos. Vasco hung his jaw open and pretended not to know a contract from a smoked ham. This conversation took place in Seville. Magellan's party had moved there soon after the signing of the contract. They were lodging at an inn a little way from the river where the ships were being fitted out. There were strips of bacon and big hams hanging from the rafters in the room where the cooking and eating went on. Vasco spent most of this meeting with Alvarez in staring stupidly at the rafters. The rest of the time he was eating. Alvarez was paying for the dinner — out of pure friendliness, of course — because it made him so happy to see a Portuguese face, he said.

He expressed great sadness that Senhor Magellan was not there — although he had watched him ride off down the river. He had a purse with gold in it, and while he asked Vasco questions about the contract, he kept clinking the coins against each other. Once he spilled some out and they rolled over to Vasco's place. Vasco picked them up and handed them back politely and went on with his roast pork. The pork

tasted especially good to Vasco because he knew King Manuel
was paying for it.

As he left the inn Alvarez decided that he might as well
have kept his money. Young Coelho was one of the thickest-
headed louts he had ever seen, as well as one of the hungriest.
He had eaten almost a pound of cheese and more olives and
bread than Alvarez had ever seen eaten by two boys. He
evidently thought only of food and knew nothing of his master's affairs. Alvarez was angry at having wasted roast pork
and flattery on this oaf. In the meantime the oaf, full of pork,
pickled pears, chestnut pudding, cream, and other trifles too
numerous to mention, was telling Magellan all about it.
Magellan took it calmly.

'That's nothing new,' he said, looking up from the endless
lists of supplies that he was always working over. 'Aranda
tells me that our late gracious master, King Manuel, even
threatened not to marry the sister of Don Carlos if he insisted
on sending ships to the Spice Islands.'

'How old is she?' Vasco asked.

'Oh, a suitable age for a third wife — about thirty years
younger than he — a little older than his daughter.'

Vasco said, 'Well, that would be a piece of luck for her —
if he didn't marry her.'

'Unfortunately for Dona Leonora it was only a threat.
Then, Aranda says, they decided they had better bribe me
to go back to Portugal, and if I refused they would consider
having me assassinated. In the meantime Alvarez had orders
to delay our sailing all he can. I think your dinner with
Alvarez means they are beginning with the bribes. I hope
you will have others with him. Eat all you can, Vasco. It
sounds to me as if Don Manuel were feeding you well.'

'It's the best meal I ever had that Manuel paid for,' Vasco
chuckled.

Alvarez did his best to delay the sailing of the fleet. It was
due to his industry that the trouble about the flags took place.
It was a clear, crisp October morning in 1518. The ships —

They were old ships and needed patching and caulking, but to Magellan and to Vasco they looked splendid....

there were five of them — were being repaired. They were
old ships and needed patching and caulking, but to Magellan
and to Vasco they looked splendid, even when they were
lying on their sides on the sands with the caulkers pounding
with their mallets and the smoke from hot pitch rising straight
into the sunshine.

The biggest ship was the Santo Antonio. Next was the
Trinidad. Smaller — and both about the same size — were
the Concepcion and the Victoria. Smallest of all was the
Santiago. Magellan had chosen the Trinidad for his flagship,
and on this particular morning he had given orders for the
royal standard, which she carried, to be repainted. It was
not bright enough to be carried at the Trinidad's masthead,
he thought.

The big flag was spread out in the sunshine on some boards
and the painter began work on it with his sponges and pans
of bright color. He had already finished the captain's flag
with Magellan's arms on it, and had made a neat job of the
red-checked bars that ran across the shield and of the eagle
with spread wings above it.

Magellan was pleased with it and ordered it hoisted on the
capstan, the correct position for it when the ship was beached.

'The captain's flag looks fine,' Vasco said to the painter.

Sometimes when the painter was in good spirits he would
let Vasco sponge on some paint. This morning, however, he
grumbled: 'It took a lot of red. Run over to the storehouse
on the quay and get me some more powdered red. Bring the
jar. You saw where I put it yesterday, didn't you?'

Vasco ran along the sandy beach to the quay, climbed up a
ladder, and was soon in the storehouse. It did not take long
to find the paint. He tucked it under his arm and went out
on the quay again. There had been only a few idlers on it
when he went in. Now there was a crowd. It seemed to have
appeared out of nowhere. Alvarez was in the centre of it.

This was not the crowd that gathered every day to watch
the work on the ships. The loafers of Seville were no different

from loafers anywhere else. They enjoyed loafing more if they could watch someone else work. They watched quietly and thoroughly for hours at a time.

This crowd was different. It moved fast along the quay. It buzzed like a swarm of bees. There were women in it, so at times there were sounds like sea gulls crying when someone throws out some dead fish. There were small boys who tripped people up, so there were curses from people who did not like being tripped. One of them was the fat Alcalde of the port. His face was an ugly plum color as he stumbled against Vasco. 'Get out of my way,' he growled, and hurried after Alvarez. 'Where is this flag?' he said to King Manuel's agent.

Alvarez pointed to the flag with Magellan's arms on it. A breeze had come up and it was flapping and snapping crisply.

'Is that indeed the ensign of Portugal?' asked the Alcalde.

'It certainly looks like it,' Alvarez said calmly.

He was lying, Vasco knew, but the crowd believed him and began to mutter angrily.

'Of course to me it is a pleasure to see it,' Alvarez added, 'but it is certainly strange that your King's flag is not displayed above it.'

Someone in the crowd shouted, 'Tear it down!' Others took up the cry and repeated it until everyone was saying it.

'Well, tear it down, then!' the Alcalde roared suddenly.

In a moment the whole crowd was off the quay and running across the sand to the Trinidad. Vasco ran with them. The stopper of the paint jar had come loose and the red powder was puffing out as he ran, but he did not know it. He ran ahead of the crowd, and found his master in the cabin. 'They are coming to tear your flag down,' he panted.

Magellan was as calm as if it were perfectly natural for Vasco to arrive powdered as red as any Indian with a roaring mob behind him. When the Alcalde and his followers arrived, Magellan was there to meet them.

'Take down that Portuguese flag,' the Alcalde puffed, looking more purple than ever.

'The flag bears my own arms,' Magellan answered quietly.
'They are properly displayed. This ship is my flagship under
commission of our royal master Don Carlos. As his captain
general I ask you to call off the men who are climbing on my
ship, and take them with you when you go.'

'Arrest this Portuguese traitor!' the Alcalde shouted.

There were plenty of men in the crowd to obey his orders,
but just at that moment Matianzo, one of the India House
officials, arrived. He asked Magellan courteously to remove
his flag, so that the crowd would go away quietly, and Magellan ordered the flag removed.

'Now,' said Matianzo to the Alcalde, 'explain, please, why
you threatened to arrest a man who has orders from the King
and from India House to get a fleet ready for sea.'

The Alcalde only muttered and growled.

Magellan said clearly, 'If you and your men do not leave
my ship at once and allow the work on it to proceed, I will
leave the ship to be tossed about by the rising tide, and you
can explain to our King why his flagship is damaged.'

In spite of Magellan's quiet way of speaking, the Alcalde
seemed to understand at last that it was he, not Magellan,
who was in trouble. He left the ship, called off his men, and
trudged back to the quay, where Alvarez was still standing,
apparently taking no interest in what went on. Alvarez, of
course, had stirred up the trouble, but it was the unlucky Alcalde who was punished When India House reported the
matter to the King, the Alcalde was soon an alcalde no
longer.

As for Vasco, it was some time before he got the red powder
all brushed out of his hair and clothes and washed out of the
creases in his hands. It would be a still longer time before he
or Magellan trusted that friendly and charming gentleman,
Sebastian Alvarez.

In August, 1519, in spite of all Alvarez could do, the ships
were ready. He knew they were, yet he made one last attempt
to turn Magellan from his plan. The man whom Manuel had

sent limping out of his presence had become an important person in Portugal. Every letter that da Costa, the Portuguese Ambassador, wrote to King Manuel had something about Magellan in it. There were long letters from Alvarez, too. He sat up late one summer night in 1519, writing one.

It was already late in the evening when Alvarez had arrived at Magellan's lodgings. Alvarez knocked and whistled while he stood waiting. He had climbed the stairs after looking contemptuously along the shabby street with its hungry, prowling cats, its dogs fighting over a duck's head, its sellers of tired-looking fruit and fish, and its drunken sailors. It was a hot, noisy street. There seemed to be at least one baby crying in every house. There was one wailing fretfully in the inn where Magellan lodged.

Alvarez knocked again. There are many kinds of knocks — timid, respectful, commanding, impatient. This was a patronizing, but impatient, knock. It said: 'Come, Come! It isn't every evening that a King's factor in his best clothes troubles to knock at the door of a runaway sea captain who lives in over a dirty tavern in a dirty street! Don't keep me waiting, please!'

Vasco opened the door. Alvarez pushed past him stating loudly, 'Your master's here. I saw him go up,' and was in the room before Vasco could bar the way.

Alvarez was all smiles as he entered the room. Magellan was on his knees, packing some dried fruits for the journey. The wailing baby was young Rodrigo Magellan, four months old. Beatriz Magellan had him in her arms. He was a thin, pale baby with eyes too large for his face, a mouth like a black cave when he cried, and a lot of straight black hair.

Alvarez thought him very handsome — he said. 'A splendid little fellow — what a noble forehead! Like his father's. Ah, there's a fine brain behind that brow. It is certainly a privilege to see him. What great things he is heir to! Islands still to be found and vast riches, I hear. His name? Rodrigo? A fine name. And he will be governor some day of those distant lands. Well, well, that's a very interesting thought. You must hate to leave him, Senhor Magellan.'

Magellan said nothing and went on packing raisins. Alvarez paid some more compliments. His idea was that if he said enough flattering things, some of them would be swallowed. However, Beatriz Magellan soon tired of them. She carried Rodrigo away to the bedroom. They could hear her walking up and down and singing to the baby in her tired, sweet voice.

Vasco had been helping with the packing when Alvarez knocked. At a sign from his master he knelt down and went to work again.

Alvarez sat in the only chair and looked on benevolently. 'If we were alone —' he said gently after a while.

'You may speak freely before my secretary,' Magellan said, beginning work on some prunes.

Alvarez smiled at the idea of the half-witted Coelho being a secretary and began to talk. Alvarez had a sweet and musical voice. It was at its sweetest as he spoke of the many and interesting talks he and Magellan had had together about this voyage.

'It seems sad,' he said with a sigh like the low note of a flute, 'that this may be our last talk. I shall miss these evenings.'

Magellan said nothing and his visitor changed from his pathetic tone to one full of vigor and frankness.

'It's a pity,' he said, 'that you pursue this road, for it has as many dangers as Saint Catherine's wheel. Now, a mutiny, for instance. Very unpleasant. Sometimes even the important men on a ship are less loyal than they seem. They may even be sent to make trouble. Dangerous, you know, very dangerous. You ought to leave the crooked road, Senhor. Take the straight road — the road to Coimbra, as we say in Portugal. Return to your own country where His Royal Highness, our great King, will most certainly shower you with favors.'

'That,' said Magellan, neatly packing jars of preserved

pears into a basket, 'would be most generous of His Highness. And if he forgot to shower me with favors I could, of course, always get seven yards of black serge and a string of acorn beads and become a hermit.'

'That is true and shows your heart is in the right place,' said Alvarez, who always laughed at his own wit and did not understand that a man with a solemn face might be making fun of him.

'Do you know what special favors His Majesty is planning for me?' Magellan inquired. 'It would be pleasant to know.'

Alvarez cleared his throat. 'Ahem, well, not definitely. It is scarcely for me to say. But it will certainly be something splendid.'

Magellan thanked him and began to pack some marmalade.

Alvarez went away before long and wrote King Manuel a letter describing this visit and giving the King the idea that Magellan would probably give up the voyage at the last minute and that if this happened it would be because Sebastian Alvarez had been so clever.

'The ships are rotten,' Alvarez said in his letter to the King. 'They will probably sink before they have been at sea many days. Also there will certainly be a mutiny. There are men in the fleet who pretend to be Magellan's friends who will really work against him. I told him this. He seemed to pay no attention, but I think his sleep will be uneasy. Do not worry about Ruy Faleiro. He is crazy. Besides, Don Carlos has ordered him to stay in Spain. He can do nothing. He is of no account. Magellan is the one we should fear.'

Even liars tell the truth sometimes. In this letter Alvarez told some things that were true.

After Alvarez had gone Magellan finished his packing. All he said to Vasco about Alvarez, his threats and promises, was: 'I think I shall keep my sailor's coat of blue serge. I feel it will suit me better than black — with acorns.'

'You'll wear cloth of gold, Senhor, before long,' Vasco said.

Beatriz Magellan had come back into the room. Rodrigo

had fallen asleep in her arms. 'He will be a big boy when you
come home,' she said softly.

Magellan touched his son's black hair with one of his hard
brown fingers. He took the baby out of his mother's arms so
gently that Rodrigo never stirred.

'What shall I bring him?' Magellan said softly. 'A monkey? He's like a monkey himself — and like me, too — isn't
he? A toy ship to sail? They say Don Carlos had a fine rock-
ing-horse when he was a boy. Shall I find one for Rodrigo,
finely carved, dapple gray, with a mane and tail of real hair
and harnessed with scarlet leather and golden bells?'

'Bring yourself,' Vasco heard Beatriz Magellan say.

She sounded sad. That was foolish. The months would slip
away . . . It was almost two years since he said good-bye to
Maria da Sousa and she would not tell him what to bring her.
It had not seemed long.

ON THE ninth of August, the Church of Santa Maria de la
Vittoria was crowded with people. Mass was being said for
the crews of Magellan's ships. They would sail down the
Guadalquivir River when the tide turned. Every bale and
bag and basket was on board. Vasco's head was still dizzy
from checking the long lists of supplies. The voice of the priest
seemed to come to him through the sound of waves whispering
along a sandy beach. The smoke from the candles was like
sea fog.

Through it he could see his master holding the King's flag.
His head cleared as Magellan in his deep, clear voice pledged
to the King his loyal service. Then the captains of the other
four ships, all taller and handsomer men than Magellan,
knelt and swore their loyalty to him. Vasco could not hear
in their voices the earnestness that rang in Magellan's. Was
one of them a traitor, as Alvarez had hinted?

Vasco looked at Juan de Cartagena, the Captain of the
Santo Antonio. Kneeling, Cartagena was not much shorter
than Magellan standing. Cartagena was broad as well as tall.
He had a broad, red face with little darting gray eyes. His
chin had fair hair on it. His mouth was always twisted a little
to one side as if he were amused at something. He went
quickly through the oath in a high voice that seemed too small
for him. He looked not at Magellan, but somewhere over his
left shoulder.

Luiz de Mendoza, who commanded the Victoria, was a
dark, grave man with a low voice. He looked at Magellan
as if he did not see him. He had already — even before the
ships sailed — refused to carry out an order of Magellan's.

He had been rebuked by Don Carlos for disobedience. Now he promised to obey. Perhaps he meant it.

Captain Gaspar Quesada of the Concepcion had a curly brown beard, which covered most of his face. The part of his face that showed was yellow and so were the whites of his brown eyes. He wore velvet and fur and shivered, although the day was warm. He stammered as he made his pledge.

The Captain of the little Santiago was Juan Serrano, a pleasant, sunburned man in clothes that had already been splashed by salt spray. Vasco noticed his bright blue eyes and wondered if he looked like his brother Francisco — the friend to whom they were sailing 'not by way of Portugal' but west through Spanish waters. Captain Serrano had a loud voice on the deck of his ship. He began to speak at the top of it, but, embarrassed by hearing it ring through the church, he dropped it and finished his oath of loyalty in a hoarse whisper.

Faleiro's pale face seemed to float suddenly out of the incense smoke. A gleam of sunshine, coming through a barred window, touched it. There was a pattern of bars across his face. With his wild eyes darting from one face to another as the captains made their vows, he was like an angry hawk in a cage.

He had pretended not to be angry when he had heard, a few days before, that the King had ordered him not to sail with the fleet. 'I shall sail with a much larger fleet. I, Sir Ruy Faleiro, Knight of Saint James, will be the supreme commander,' he had said, and snapped his thin fingers and laughed.

Today he looked gay no longer. His lips moved as Magellan spoke and there was an angry gleam in his eyes.

'It is as if he were cursing us,' Vasco thought with a shudder. 'Well, at least he is not going with us.'

Behind Faleiro, gaily dressed in crimson silk and looking very hot in it, was young Signor Antonio Pigafetta, a Knight of Rhodes. Signor Antonio had a very strong desire, he had told Don Carlos, to see what he called 'the very great and awful things of ocean.' The King had given him permission to sail with Magellan.

Vasco had already seen the Knight of Rhodes on board the Trinidad. Pigafetta had been in every corner of each of the ships and had seen everything there was to see with his little green eyes. He asked questions faster than they could be answered, but that did not matter, as he often gave the answers himself. He believed everything he heard and some things he didn't and he was planning to write a book. He was always scribbling things on scraps of paper and losing them, or sharpening the point of a quill and then sticking it behind his ear and forgetting it, or getting ink on his fingers and rubbing it on his face.

He was a round young man with a turned-up nose and a wide mouth. He was smoothly shaven and his reddish-brown hair was brushed neatly back from his forehead. That is, it was neatly brushed that day; Signor Antonio had a habit of rumpling it while he was writing, so on most days it hung over his eyes.

Vasco liked Signor Antonio Pigafetta and was glad he was sailing with the fleet, but suddenly he forgot all about him. There was a tall man in black standing behind the Knight of Rhodes and beside him was a girl in green and silver, a girl with brown curls who was looking at Vasco. 'Now what,' he thought, 'is Maria da Sousa doing here?'

Then he remembered that she was a niece of the wife of Senhor da Costa, the Portuguese Ambassador, the man beside whom she was standing.

'We are enemies now,' he thought.

Maria, however, did not seem to know it. She was standing on the steps of the church when he came out. All the grand people had come out ahead. Vasco was one of the last to leave. His eyes were dazzled by the bright sunshine after the dimness of the church. Perhaps that was why Maria looked so pretty. She was taller than he remembered and her freckles were gone — all but three on her nose. He had never noticed her dimples before — at least he didn't think he had — nor how long her eyelashes were. He had a good chance to look at them because she lowered her eyelids when he spoke to her. He wondered why she was there alone. Nieces of ambassadors did not stand alone on church steps in strange cities.

'What are you doing here?' he asked.

'Oh,' said Maria, 'it really is you. I thought it was — when I saw your feet. Thank you for your kind welcome to Spain. I am lost. I was with my uncle. I got separated from him in the crowd.'

'I'll take you home,' Vasco said.

'Isn't your ship going to sail?'

'Soon. When the tide turns. But I can run back.'

The walk to the Ambassador's palace seemed short, perhaps because Maria was telling Vasco all about things at home.

'King Manuel is angry with you,' she said after she had answered questions about Vasco's family.

'Splendid! — Why?'

'Because you are going on this crazy voyage, of course. He knows you will never come back.'

'He must be breaking his heart about that,' Vasco said. 'Isn't there anyone to spill soup in his lap now?'

Maria giggled. 'The Princess is really sorry,' she said. 'Must you go, Vasco? My uncle is going to Lisbon soon. You could travel with us. Angela Luisa wants you to come home for her wedding. I am to be a bridesmaid. Do you have to take such long steps?'

Vasco slowed down and said: 'I'm sorry. And sorry not to be at the wedding. Will you wear that dress? It's very pretty.'

'How stupid men are! I shall have a new dress, of course. I suppose all you know is the price of salt beef and rope. I hear you are one of the most important men in the fleet. They say Captain Magellan couldn't do without you.'

Vasco was pleased at being called a man even if he was considered a stupid one. 'Nonsense,' he said, blushing. 'Why, they even got my name wrong on the list of the crew. I saw a copy of it which had been made for His Majesty and I was going to correct it, but when I came back with the pen, someone had already sent it away. They wrote my name down as "Vasco Gomez Gallego" instead of "Vasco da Gama Coelho." That shows you how important I am. There was a pilot of that name and someone confused us.'

Maria changed the subject, 'If you saw that a friend of yours was going to throw himself into the river, would you do something that seemed mean or — well — rough, perhaps, to save him from drowning?'

'Snatch him out by the hair, you mean? Why, if I knew he couldn't swim, I might, I suppose. But if I knew he could look after himself, I'd let him alone. He might not thank me for interfering. Men hate to have people act as if they didn't trust them.'

'Oh!' Maria said. 'Well, there is my uncle's house. You had better go now. Good-bye. I am afraid you will miss your boat. No, don't come any farther. Hurry! Hurry!'

Vasco was puzzled by being hurried off. First she said he had walked too fast. Now she wanted him to run — and he didn't want to run. A sudden wave of homesickness came over him.

'You never told me what to bring you,' he said. 'That morning. You were going to, but you didn't.'

But she did not tell him this time either. She had already slipped through the gate of the Ambassador's garden. It clanged behind her, leaving him standing there. He stood looking up at the house only half-seeing it. A window opened above his head and Maria came out on a small balcony.

Maria did not speak. She had a strange look on her face. She made a sign with her hands as if she were pushing him away and when he did not move, she stamped her foot at his stupidity. Then the gate clanged again and four men in the Ambassador's red and light blue liveries came out. One of them stepped up to Vasco

'The Ambassador wishes to speak to you, Senhor,' he said.

He spoke politely, but there was something threatening in the looks of the others. One of them had his hand on his dagger.

Vasco understood suddenly. The Ambassador had told Maria to bring him to the palace so that he could be seized and sent back to Portugal. It was a trick to hurt Magellan. Only when it came to the point Maria couldn't lead him into the trap. Perhaps it had seemed like a game to her at first, but at last she had known it was treachery.

It was all clear in Vasco's mind as he bowed courteously. 'I thank you. Lead the way to His Excellency,' he said.

The men turned. Vasco looked up once more at Maria. She was still pointing towards the river. Vasco waved to her, spun around, and ran down the street.

The Ambassador's footmen were chosen for their fine appearance rather than for speed of either feet or brains. They all had hearty appetites and they had been called away from a haunch of boiled mutton. One of them still had a chunk of it stuffed in one cheek. He got a stitch in his side almost at once. Another stubbed his toe on a stone and fell heavily. The things he said as he got up, dusting his knees, were greatly enjoyed by the small boys who had appeared from nowhere, as small boys do when there is something going on. Some of them joined in the chase and got in the way of the third footman so that he stumbled into a hole and wrenched his ankle. It was painful and he decided that a cup of wine would make it feel better.

The fourth man was a better runner than the others. He was heavy but he had long legs. Vasco looked back once and saw that the man was catching up on him. Vasco ran faster but he could still hear the thudding footsteps. No matter how fast he ran, they were still close behind him.

Vasco turned suddenly and ran up a narrow street, then swung left into another. For a minute he thought he had escaped. Then he heard the pounding feet again. The street he was on now — like many other streets in Seville — led to the Guadalquivir. Vasco slowed down and began to limp. He put his hand to his side gasping.

He and the footman were alone in this short street, which sloped down to the riverbank. No one had noticed the runners yet. The shouts of the crowd were still in the distance.

The footsteps behind Vasco were quicker now. It was easy running for the Ambassador's man, because the street sloped so sharply. He'd have the limping boy in a minute, he thought. He'd catch him in sight of the ships of that traitor Magellan, drag him home, get the gold piece the Ambassador had promised if the boy was captured.

The footman was already planning how to spend the gold piece. He'd dine on roast duckling and red wine. He'd buy a ribbon and a string of beads for the kitchenmaid. There would still be silver to clink in his purse, he thought, and stretched out his hand for the runaway's collar. Just at that moment Vasco started running again. The footman cursed and lengthened his stride.

'I'll get him when he turns at the riverbank,' he thought, and ran faster.

Only Vasco did not turn at the riverbank. Just as the fat red hand shot out again and snatched at his shoulder, Vasco sprang into the air and dove cleanly into the green waters of the Guadalquivir. In the moment before he struck the water a pleasant sound came to his ears. It was the Ambassador's footman rolling down the bank into the river. When Vasco came to the surface and shook the water out of his eyes, the footman was wallowing out of the water. Vasco felt sorry not to stay and enjoy the footman's bath. However, the noise of his roars and snorts as he tried to get the slippery green water weeds off his face gave a great deal of happiness to the small boys, who had now arrived at the river.

'Look at the whale on the beach!' one of them shouted.

'That's no whale!' yelled another. 'That's a hippopotamus. My father, he's been in Africa. He says they snort like that.'

'It's Neptune, *I* think,' said one who was having the advantage of a classical education. 'That's one of his dolphins swimming away from him. Hi, Neptune, hurry and catch that dolphin. He's getting away!'

By this time the 'dolphin' was halfway out to the anchored ships of Magellan's fleet. The sailors were leaning over the bulwarks and adding their shouts to the general uproar. The crowd on the quay, waiting for the tide to turn and the ships to leave, shouted too. When Vasco reached the Trinidad's side and was hauled up on a rope thrown to him by one of the sailors, the shouts were louder than ever. By then the Ambassador's footman had scraped most of the weeds off himself and was walking home with all the dignity that a man can show when the red of his livery is running into the blue and his stockings are coming down. His young admirers had thought it wise to leave when he began to climb the bank. So he walked alone.

'That this should happen to me, Duarte Alvarez,' he thought bitterly. 'My cousin Sebastian and his schemes! Yes, he's the great man of our family and I'm only a footman. I wish I had him out in the river with me. I'd show him what I think of him . . .'

When he got home Duarte was scolded by the Ambassador, and scolded even more loudly than the others because he had come the nearest to catching Vasco. Duarte considered this unfair — as indeed it was — and he was extremely ill-tempered at supper that night.

So was the Ambassador. His niece had brought the Portuguese traitor Coelho back to the palace according to her uncle's suggestion — all for the foolish boy's good, of course — and then had disappeared. The Ambassador had gone out to look for her, but after an hour's aimless pacing of the streets, he had come home and found her sitting in the garden sewing and wondering why her dear uncle was late to supper.

He decided not to ask her any questions. He disliked looking ridiculous and something about Maria's eyes made him uneasy. He would say nothing, he decided. He said nothing in a marked way all through supper and scowled at the unfortunate Duarte, who told Caterina, the kitchenmaid, that he intended to sail to the Americas. He would probably marry an Indian princess, he said. Caterina cried and let the rice scorch, and what the cook said when she came back into the kitchen did not make the evening any pleasanter.

However, Duarte did not go to the Americas. He married Caterina after all, and they went home to Lisbon and started a small inn. Caterina became famous for ducklings stuffed with chestnuts, pancakes with honey and thick cream, and a special way of cooking sardines. Duarte got so fat that he never thought of running even six steps. He was really a good-natured man, especially after a large dinner, so as time went on he used to laugh about his plunge in the river. It was one of his favorite stories. Caterina used to ask him not to tell it oftener than once a week. . . .

On the Trinidad no one had time to scold Vasco. The strong tide in the Guadalquivir turned soon after he reached the Trinidad and there was all the bustle of setting sails to catch every breath of the light breeze and hauling up the anchors. It was all strange and exciting to Vasco — the shouts of the sailors, the cries from on land, the moment when the Trinidad first began to move, and when the figures on the quay a little way down the river suddenly grew clearer.

Vasco saw Sebastian Alvarez standing stiff and straight among the waving hands. 'He's hoping we'll sink,' Vasco thought. 'It's strange to be seen off only by someone who's wishing you bad luck. There's no one else I know there, not even Faleiro.'

Just then there was a movement in the crowd. Someone wiggled through it and reached the end of the quay. Vasco saw a green dress and a bunch of brown curls. The Trinidad passed so near that the little packet she tossed him fell easily at his feet.

He heard her call: 'Good luck, Vasco. May Saint Christopher guard and keep you. Come safe home.'

The Trinidad slipped past the quay. The brightly dressed people on it ceased to look like people and became a flower garden with a breeze blowing through it. Soon Maria's face was only one of the pink spots among the other colors. Vasco turned the packet over in his cold fingers. They were still blue from his swim. It was a square of green silk like Maria's dress. She had tied the corners together and then tied a silver ribbon tightly around it. Inside was something hard that clinked.

It was a heavy gold chain, he found, when he had untied the knots. With it was a note, hastily scrawled and blotted.

The chain on your locket is wearing out. This was my father's. It will be better. I will run with it to the dock, but if they catch me, I will send it to San Lucar. You asked me what I wanted you to bring me. I don't care what you bring — if you bring it.

MARIA

It had taken him longer to read than he thought. He looked back at the quay, but the figures on it were so small that he could not see which was Maria. He need not have strained his eyes. Maria was already running back to the Ambassador's palace, so that she could be sitting quietly in the garden in case he wanted to see her.

The smells of the hot city blew away in the freshening breeze. From a warehouse on the riverbank came the scent of cloves and cinnamon.

'The next time I smell them,' Vasco thought, 'I'll be in the Spice Islands.'

SIGNOR ANTONIO PIGAFETTA felt the motion of the ship a little, he said. Sailors on the Trinidad grinned and said Signor Antonio was seasick. Certainly that young knight was already finding out some of 'the very great and awful things of ocean.' For the first part of the voyage he lay in his bunk and looked at the ocean as little as possible. He said there was too much of it. 'And it's all water,' he complained to Vasco.

However, before many days Signor Antonio felt well enough to dictate his account of the first part of the voyage to Vasco. Pigafetta had promised the Grand Master of Rhodes to keep a diary. He had already written several pages of fine long words explaining how he happened to join Magellan.

'I will not tell the Grand Master about our fleet,' Pigafetta said. 'It is not necessary to mention this strange sickness that has come upon me, because as the days go on, it seems likely that I shall live, although at first I hoped to die. Keep your quill cut, boy, and hold your paper steady, for I notice that when I wrote it seemed to slide away from me. Now begin.

'The Captain General, Ferdinand Magellan, would not begin this voyage of ours without making some good rules. This is the custom of those of us who go to sea. (The Grand Master has never sailed except in the Mediterranean and such small waters. Of the Ocean Sea he knows nothing. Take more

ink. . . .) His rules were needed because there are impetuous
storms on this ocean. Besides, the captains and masters of
the other ships do not love him. Perhaps this is because he is
Portuguese and they are Spaniards. Portuguese and Spaniards have ill-will against each other. Still these men are
obedient to him. . . .

'Why do you think these men dislike the Captain General,
Vasco?' Pigafetta asked.

'Perhaps for the reason you say, Signor. Perhaps because
they are cowards and traitors. He has been warned more than
once that there are traitors in the fleet, but he pays no attention. He says a fleet without traitors is like a dog without
fleas.'

'Why?'

'Because there is no such thing as a dog without fleas. Or if
there is, it isn't a dog.'

'Humph!' snorted Pigafetta. 'One of those fleas, I'll wager
my best belt — which is now somewhat too large — is that
crook-mouthed Cartagena. Wasn't he the one who failed to
salute the Captain General last evening? I heard something
about it. If I were the Captain I'd trust Cartagena with one
of my ships no more than I would a cat with a kettle of fish
stew. Still, I'm not Captain... Take more ink... and
write.

'The Captain General ordered that his own ship should go
ahead and for the others to follow it. At night he carries a
torch of burning wood on the poop. It burns all night so that
the lookouts on the other ships can see it and follow. Sometimes he uses a lantern or a thick cord of reeds. They soak
the reeds in water first. Then they beat them and twist them
together and dry them in the sun. They burn well.

'The other ships answer his signals. If he changes his tack,
he shows two lights. If he lowers his small sail, he shows three
lights. Four if he lowers the large sail. Five if he sees land or
a rock.

'He ordered three watches kept at night. The first from

sunset to midnight. The next from midnight till dawn, and the third beginning at dawn. We sailors call this the Star of Break of Day watch. The crews of all the ships are divided into watches. The first is the captain's watch, the second the pilot's, and the third is the master's ...

'Who is that little fat black boy in your watch, Vasco? The one who sings out the calls like a nightingale?' Pigafetta asked.

'Juan de Santandres is his name,' Vasco said, laying down his pen.

'I saw him crying this morning. He's no nightingale when he howls. What is wrong with him?' Pigafetta asked.

'I suppose there is always a bully on a ship,' Vasco said, taking out his knife and fixing the point on his quill. 'This one is Simon, that handsome light-haired boy, who serves our meals. '

'I noticed he had a black eye at dinner.'

'Did you? I didn't look at him.'

Pigafetta began to laugh. 'He looked at you often enough. I thought he was going to pour the stew down your neck. Come, Vasco, you might as well tell me about it. Because I'll find out anyway.'

'It was only about some lemons,' Vasco said. 'I don't think handsome Simon will steal any more for a while. My pen is ready now, Signor Antonio.'

'Good. Whose lemons were they? Tell me the story. Think how sadly ill I have been! I thought we were friends. Were they Juan's?'

'Yes. They belonged to Juan. His mother was a cook at an inn in Seville. We stayed there. His father died long ago and the mother was very ill. She had some kind of fever and a bad cough. She died just before we sailed, but before that she had asked the Captain if Juan could go with us. Senhor Magellan said "Yes" and she was happy about it. I think she knew she was going to die. She had not been able to work for some weeks before we sailed, but she sewed shirts and jerkins for

Juan and did everything to get him ready. With some of the
last money she earned she bought him a chest for his things.
It was just a cheap box with rope handles, but it had a lock.
She kept the key around her neck till the last. As long as she
could walk she'd go out to the shops and buy little things and
pack them in it.'

'Lemons?'

'Yes, and other things. Raisins, dried apricots. Jars of
preserves. A silk handkerchief. Oranges. Honey. The gold
rings his father used to wear in his ears. Juan said she would
never let him see what she put in. She showed them to me,
though. It was all to be a surprise for Juan. She came from
the Canary Islands. She told Juan not to open the box until
after we had left there. She thought it would make the voyage
seem shorter, I suppose.'

'He was counting the days, of course.'

'Yes. And when we left Teneriffe he went down to open the
chest. He was too late. Somehow Simon had found out about
it. He'd broken the lock and he and some of his friends were
sucking oranges and eating figs and throwing lemons to each
other. Simon was juggling with three of them and he had the
silk handkerchief tied on his head and the rings in his ears.
They'd tossed the shirts and things around and broken a jar
of marmalade over the stockings she'd knitted.'

'Ah,' Pigafetta said. 'This is making me angry. I think I
must find some necks and wring them, but you have attended
to that, no doubt.'

'No. I was gentle with them. Three of them ran away when
they saw me.'

'I can't think why,' chuckled Pigafetta.

'That left only Simon and a little rat whose name I do not
know. They arranged such things as they had not eaten or
soiled neatly in the chest again. Simon washed the jerkin and
dried it. He is a better laundress than you would think to look
at him. Shall I take more ink?'

'You shall not. You stood and looked at these gentlemen
and they repacked the chest — that was it, was it?'

'Why, yes.'

Pigafetta turned around suddenly.

'Was that it, Juan?' he said to the little negro.

'How long have you been listening, you little scamp?'
Vasco asked good-naturedly.

'He's been standing in the door since you were telling about
Simon washing the jerkin. So Senhor Vasco just stood there
looking at them and they put everything away — was that it,
Juan?'

'Well, Signor Pigafetta, yes. Only first Don Vasco ——'

'Senhor Vasco will do for the present,' Vasco suggested.

'Well, Signor Pigafetta, first he came in and — wham! —
he knocked down that little Juan Martin, who lies on the floor
for quite a time saying nothing. So then Don — I mean
Senhor — Vasco, he takes that Simon thief by the back of his
neck. No, first he fist-fights with him a little, then he takes
him by the neck and he says, "You like lemons, do you?"
And he picks up half one some of them had cut and he slams it
in that Simon's mouth. Then he says, "Your face needs
washing" and he washes it. Don Vasco does, with the other
half of the lemon. Then he made them pick up the things, and
told them to carry the chest in here. If Don Vasco ——'

'Senhor Vasco . . .'

'Excuse me, please. Senhor Vasco. If he wasn't sitting on
it, I would be much pleased to offer you something out of it,
Signor Antonio.'

'Thank you, Juan. Another day, perhaps, when I feel
stronger. I have not been feeling well today. Something I
ate, probably.'

'As a matter of fact,' Signor Antonio said when Juan had
trotted off with his mouth full of apricots, 'I feel very well.
My health has always been perfect. It seemed too bad that
the boy should be robbed by me as well as by those —— Well,
it's over. Let us be calm. Take more ink — and write:

'We sailed from Seville down the Guadalquivir on Monday,
the tenth of August, and passing by many small villages we

arrived at a castle which belongs to the Duke of Medina
Sidonia. There is a port there from which you enter the Ocean
Sea. You go into the harbor by the east wind and out by the
west wind. We stayed many days in the port and went every
day to hear Mass at the Church of Our Lady of Barrameda
near San Lucar.

'We were waiting for some things we needed for our voyage.'

Pigafetta paused here and asked, 'Was it at San Lucar that
the Captain General received the King's letter?'

'I am not sure. I saw him reading some of it at San Lucar.
I don't think he read it all. It was seventy pages long.'

'I suppose it contained much good advice.'

'Why, yes, for a man who has never been to sea Don Carlos
has many good ideas,' Vasco answered. 'He said the crews
must not quarrel, or gamble, or use bad language. If they are
sick, the Captain must pay them kindly visits. He told Captain Magellan that there was a right and a wrong way of drop-
ping anchors.'

Vasco had been giving this account of the King's letter with
a serious face, but at the snort Pigafetta gave on hearing that
the King was teaching Magellan how to drop anchor, he could
not help laughing.

Signor Antonio chuckled and remarked: 'I suppose the Captain General is so busy tucking the crew into bed that he cannot pay me kindly visits while I am wasting away here. Let
me see — did the King say anything about washing the
crew's faces with lemon juice? Did he tell the Captain not to
let them get their feet wet?'

'No,' Vasco replied, 'but he said they must be allowed to
write letters home whenever they liked.'

Pigafetta chuckled some more.

'And if they drop the letters in the sea, I suppose the sharks
will carry them back to Spain. Your King thinks of every·
thing. Well, that's better than thinking of nothing. You are a
young scamp to laugh at His Majesty.'

'I wasn't laughing — you were,' Vasco stated untruthfully,

'Perhaps,' said Pigafetta with great dignity, *'you had better take more ink —*
thank you — and write...'

and then added seriously, 'There's no other king in the world fit to make a doormat for Don Carlos — even if he hasn't sailed the Ocean Sea. And if he did I'm sure he wouldn't be seasick.'

'Perhaps,' said Pigafetta with great dignity, 'you had better take more ink — thank you — and write:

'On Tuesday, the twentieth of September, 1519, we set sail from San Lucar, taking a southwest course, and in six days we reached Teneriffe in the Canaries and stayed there three days taking in provisions. We also stayed two days at another port taking in pitch, which is a thing necessary for ships.'

('The cooks put it in the pudding,' said Vasco.)

'It is well known,' Pigafetta went on, 'that in the Canaries there is an island where there is not a drop of water to be found, except that once a day a great cloud falls on a large tree there. The water falls on the leaves and runs to the foot of the tree so that it is like a fountain. The men that live there enjoy this water and wild and tame animals both drink it. Unfortunately we did not visit this island, so we did not see this tree.'

'Very unfortunate indeed,' said Vasco, 'and a great pity that there is not a kind that sheds ink as well: for my ink horn is dry.'

The Knight of Rhodes then threw a pillow at the Captain General's secretary. Vasco threw it back. Soon the room was full of feathers and Signor Antonio was sneezing.

That day there was no more writing in his book.

EASTER IN PATAGONIA

THE pillow fight seemed to do Pigafetta good. The next day he was on deck, notebook in hand, asking the sailors questions and writing down remarkable things that they told him.

'On Monday, the third of October,' he wrote in his book, 'we set sail at midnight on a southeast course, passed the Cape Verde Islands, and sailed along the coast of Guinea in Africa. Sometimes the wind was against us, sometimes fair. Sometimes we had rain and no wind, and at one time so many bad squalls that we could no longer go forward. So, in order that the ships might not perish, we struck our sails and went here and there about the sea until fair weather came.

'Afterwards there was a great calm and large fishes called sharks swam near our ships. They have teeth of a terrible kind and when they find people in the sea, alive or dead, they eat them. Some of the men caught one and ate some of it. A shark might like to eat me, but me — I never could like shark.

'During these storms the light that sailors call Saint Elmo's fire appeared on our masthead. It stayed there two hours. The sailors said it was a good sign. It must be so, for when it went away the sea became calm. The sailors saw many kinds of birds. They say there is one kind that has no feet and another where the mother lays her eggs on the mate's back and there they are hatched. This, however, I did not see. There are also fish that fly and we saw a great many together so that it seemed we were looking at an island in the sea.

'To reach the Equator it took us sixty days, sailing south,' he wrote later. 'At last the North Star was no longer to be seen at night and we turned west towards Brazil. We are anchored in a port in that country now. The people bring us meat that seems like veal. We also trade with them for fowls and sweet fruits. For a knife they give half a dozen fowls. For a comb they give two fat geese, and for a pair of scissors or a small mirror they give so much fish that the men cannot eat it all. They gave me five fowls for the king of hearts of an old pack of playing-cards that I brought with me from Italy, and they thought they had cheated me. To another man for a mirror they gave ten parrots and some little cat monkeys, yellow like a lion and very pleasing.

'We reached here on the thirteenth of December. Brazil is a country larger than all of France, Spain, and Italy. It belongs to the King of Portugal. There are no Portuguese here at present.

'The people here often live to be a hundred years old. They wear no clothes but a few parrot's feathers, and they sleep in nets called hammocks. Their boats are dug out of the trunk of a tree and are called canoes. Their oars are like shovels. These people are not black like Africans, but rather brown. Their king is called a Cacique. I am learning some words of their language.

'They bake bread but I did not like it. They make it out of part of certain trees. The men carry bows and arrows and their wives carry their children on their backs in a net. One day a very beautiful girl came on our ship. She saw a nail about as long as her finger and took it and hid it in her hair. The Captain and I saw her hide it and then hurry away.'

It was the day they anchored in the Brazilian port that Vasco first saw the crew of the Victoria. Magellan had sent

him with a message to Captain Mendoza. Juan de Santandres, who always followed at Vasco's heels when ne saw a
chance to do so, tugged away at the bow oar of the boat that
carried Vasco to the Victoria. Juan's arms were strong but
his legs were short. It is hard to row with your feet scarcely
touching the bottom of the boat, but Juan did his best and
the boat reached the Victoria about as soon as if he had not
been there catching an occasional crab. He carried the present
— a net full of fruit — that Magellan had sent to Captain
Mendoza and followed Vasco into the cabin. Juan felt very
much pleased with himself that morning. He had on a clean
white shirt. His red handkerchief was tied over his woolly
head. His gold rings were in his ears and his white teeth shone
in a cheerful grin.

Captain Mendoza was playing cards. The man who was
playing with him had his back to the cabin door. He was a big
broad-shouldered man with a head covered with yellow curls.

Captain Mendoza tossed a queen of spades languidly on the
table, raised his heavy eyelids slowly, and drawled: 'Ah, the
Captain General's secretary. Coelho, isn't it?'

The other card-player turned his head slowly at this and
Vasco found himself looking into the glassy blue eyes of
Sebastian del Cano. Del Cano favored Vasco with one of his
bows — the tipping back of his yellow head and the drooping
of his eyelids that he used for a bow.

Vasco made the low bow that he had been taught at King
Manuel's Court, and then could have kicked himself for making it. Why didn't he have the sense to stick his chin up in
the air and squint — like del Cano?

However, he delivered his message clearly, took the net of
fruit from Juan and presented it to Captain Mendoza, accepted his languid thanks, and bowed himself out. Mendoza
had already picked up his cards again. Vasco's farewells were
made to his lowered face and del Cano's back.

The minutes spent in the cabin had seemed too long to
Vasco. He hated its stuffiness and Mendoza's weary polite·

ness, which came so near rudeness. It was worse still to find del Cano there — del Cano, whom he had last seen talking to Sebastian Alvarez the day before they sailed.

'When did he join the fleet?' he wondered, and then realized that he had spoken out loud.

They were back on the Trinidad by that time. Juan, who was close behind him as usual, said: 'You mean that fine big yellow-haired gentleman? I saw him go aboard the Victoria the night before we sailed. This the first time you saw him, Don — I mean Senhor Vasco?'

'No, but it's the first time I knew he was with the fleet. I saw him in Portugal and again in Spain.'

'Very handsome gentleman,' Juan said.

This seemed to be a question and Vasco said, 'Yes, del Cano is a fine-looking man.'

Privately he wished that this fine-looking man were on some other ship on some other ocean.

He did not see del Cano again in that port.

'We stayed thirteen days in this country of Brazil and then sailed south,' Pigafetta wrote. 'Near a great river — we thought it might be the strait we were looking for, but it was not — we saw men as great as giants. One of them came to the ship. He had a voice like a bull. Some of our men went ashore to catch him and his friends, but they ran away. They could do more at a step than our men could at a bound.

'Following our course southwards we found two islands full of geese and sea wolves. These geese are black with a white shirt in front and they do not fly, but swim in the water and waddle on land. We filled our five ships with them in an hour. One of our crew, a man who had sailed far south before, called them penguins, but I call them geese. This same fellow said the sea wolves were seals. All I can say is they bark like wolves on a frosty night. They are the size and thickness of a calf, only with small round ears. Large teeth they have, and no legs, but feet growing close to the body. These feet are like a hand, with skin growing between the fingers like a goose's feet.

I think these wolves would be bad and cruel if they could run on land, but luckily they stay in the water and catch fish.

'Now, after we had sailed south for some time we came to a harbor which we named Port St. Julian. We stayed there because in this part of the world the winter was coming on, although with you at home the longest days of the year would be just ahead. It was a lonely place and for two months we did not see any natives. Yet suddenly one day we saw a giant on the shore and he was dancing and bounding and singing. While he sang he put the sea sand on his head.

'Our Captain sent a sailor ashore and told him to leap and sing like the giant to show friendship. This sailor did this and led the giant to a place on shore where the Captain and others of us went and waited for them. The giant was astonished when he saw us and pointed to the sky with his finger. He thought we came from heaven. He was so tall that even the tallest of us — such as Sebastian del Cano, or young Coelho, who grows like a weed — came hardly above his waist.

'He had a large face painted red with yellow around his eyes. He had two hearts painted on his cheeks. His head was almost bald and was painted white. He was dressed in the skin of an animal called a guanaco. Guanacos have a head and ears like a mule, only smaller, a neck like a camel, the legs of a deer, and a tail like a horse. This giant had shoes of a guanaco's skin. He carried a short bow with arrows feathered like ours, but with cut stones instead of iron for heads.

'The Captain had food and drink brought for the giant and showed him some of our goods, among them a steel mirror. When the giant saw himself in it, he leaped backwards, knocking over three or four of our men.

'Later other giants came to the shore and we traded with them. One of them was a very gracious and amiable person who liked to dance and leap. When he leapt, the earth would sink in as much as the width of the palm of your hand. We called these natives Patagonians on account of their large feet.

'We baptized one of them with the name of John. We taught him some prayers and he learned to say them in good Latin, but in a terribly loud voice.

'Our men captured two of these giants and the Captain took them on board our ship so that he could take them back to Spain and show them to the King. At first they were angry and foamed at the mouth and cried aloud: "Setebos! Setebos!" This is the name of their god. Later they became quiet. We named one of them Paul. They liked our food and would eat a whole basketful of biscuit at a time. They caught rats on the ship and ate them without skinning. Half a bucket of water at a time was their drink...'

Seeing Vasco just then, Pigafetta threw down the pen and stretched his arms.

'Ah, here you are — all the two yards of you. Take the pen and write for me, Vasco,' he said. 'My hand is cramped. When I try to form the letters, my arm aches up to my right ear. It is a long time since you wrote for me. You are lazy. You do nothing but hunt rabbits and foxes and talk Malay with Enrique and Patagonian with the giants. You sing almost as loud as the giants do. You and that little Juan are always singing, but Juan at least sings in tune.'

'Thank you,' Vasco said.

'It is nothing. I do my best to educate you, that is all. I am older than you ——'

'Three years,' Vasco remarked, taking out his knife and beginning to cut a new pen.

'And wiser,' Pigafetta went on, 'so I give you good advice. I have had much given me at different times and as I am not using it, I present it to you.'

'Very generous of you, Signor, and I thank you,' Vasco said, clicking the pen against his thumbnail.

'Begin at the top of the page,' Pigafetta said, 'and write as follows and do not make blots... Say: "We remained in this port about five months during which strange things happened."'

'Indeed they did,' Vasco yawned, writing it down. 'Or rather they were not strange. Before we left Portugal I knew they would happen.'

'Nonsense,' said Pigafetta. 'I noticed nothing.'

'Perhaps you were too busy looking for birds without feet and whales with wings,' Vasco suggested. 'The Captain was warned of trouble before we left Portugal. We had our eyes open for something besides trees that rain, I can tell you.'

'It was lucky you were here. I do not see how Captain Magellan ever dared sail without you before,' Pigafetta said solemnly. 'I wonder how he ever got to India and back alive. You must have been at least five years old then. You ought to have gone out there and rescued him from that sandbank. The one he and Serrano were wrecked on.'

Pigafetta could not help laughing at his own wit. He got so red in the face and choked and chuckled so that Vasco began to laugh too. There was no more writing in Pigafetta's notebook that day.

It was true that Vasco had always had an uneasy feeling about Juan de Cartagena. They were not far on their voyage before Cartagena had questioned an order of Magellan's.

Magellan had replied curtly, 'Follow the flagship and ask no questions.'

This was good advice, but Cartagena was angry. He failed to obey another order. Magellan took away Cartagena's position as captain of the Santo Antonio and gave command of the ship to Alvaro Mesquita. Mesquita was a Portuguese and a cousin of Magellan's. The appointment displeased the Spaniards of the fleet.

They were no better pleased when Magellan ordered the rations of meat and biscuit reduced. By the time the fleet anchored at Port St. Julian, Magellan knew that the voyage to the Spice Islands would take far longer than he had expected. He had hoped to have found the strait before this and had planned to spend the winter on the Pacific shores of South America. Yet here it was seven months since they had left

Seville and no sign of a strait leading into the Pacific had been found.

The short Antarctic days and the long nights when the icy winds blew the sea into black mountains edged with snow were bad for exploring. It was only sensible to spend the winter in the sheltered bay and to save the beef and biscuit for the voyage ahead. They could live on fish and rabbits and the bread they had bought from the natives.

Cutting down the rations made the crews all the more ready to listen to Cartagena. He had long ago begun to tell the sailors that the strait was only a crazy dream of Magellan's. The thing to do now was to turn and sail back to Spain. There would be plenty to eat for the voyage home. Also — though Cartagena did not mention it — there would be a reward waiting for him in the purse of Sebastian Alvarez if Magellan's fleet came home without having found the western route to the Spice Islands.

'That lame monkey on the flagship will starve and drown us all if we do not make him turn back,' Cartagena said.

By Easter Sunday Cartagena had stirred up plenty of bad feeling. In St. Julian's Bay Easter was the sign that the worst part of the winter was just ahead. Already the days were short. Hunting on shore was cold work. When night came, the crews had long hours to spend, huddled into cold, stuffy quarters between decks without enough to eat. They rolled dice in the feeble light from twisted rushes stuck in an iron holder or played cards with a dirty pack that Pigafetta had given to one of them. There were quarrels over these games on most evenings, although sometimes the men were too cold and sulky even to quarrel.

On the day before Easter Magellan sent Vasco with a message to the other ships. There would be Mass celebrated on shore in the morning and the captains were asked to go to Mass with their crews. Afterwards dinner would be served on the Trinidad and Magellan invited the other captains to share it with him.

'I think they will not come, Senhor Captain,' Vasco said when he came back from the errand.

Magellan was sitting at the table studying one of Faleiro's charts. He looked up and said quietly, 'Why do you say that?'

'Captain Mendoza bowed and thanked you for your courtesy. He did not say he would come. Sebastian del Cano was with him. They were drinking together. I heard them laughing after I had left the cabin. Captain Serrano has not yet returned from exploring the coast south of the bay. He had a strong crew to row him, but they think on the Santiago that he will not return until tomorrow or even the next day. On the Concepcion Captain Quesada talked loud about how busy he was. He did not say at what, but he bellowed at the master of the ship that the crews were ordered to go on shore to Mass tomorrow. Your cousin, Captain Mesquita, accepted with pleasure.'

'Tomorrow will be a day to remember, I think,' Magellan said calmly, and went back to studying his chart.

The captains of the Concepcion and the Victoria did not go on shore to Mass, and they did not come to dinner on the Trinidad. Alvaro Mesquita from the Santo Antonio was the only guest. Mesquita was a little white-faced, nervous man. He was never good company, and on this Easter Sunday he was especially restless. He ate little, bit his fingernails, crumbled his biscuit, and spilled his wine. The dinner was good — oysters, broiled fish, stewed rabbit, some of the roots they had brought with them from Brazil. The natives called them batatas.

Magellan had given the cook some of his own supply of raisins and figs for a steamed pudding. There was a small one for the cabin and a larger one for the crew. Wine and biscuit were served to everyone that day.

Magellan ate his dinner with a good appetite.

'These batatas are good. I wonder if they would grow in Europe,' he said to Juan de Santandres, who was helping to serve. Enrique had been ill, but now he had recovered and things were pleasanter at meals. Simon had been sent to the Victoria, from which ship he had come on board the Trinidad at Teneriffe to take Enrique's place.

'Batatas grow in Europe? Certainly,' said Pigafetta, who always had opinions on every subject. 'It is very simple. Each batata has several eyes from which sprouts will grow. You cut out chunks, each of which has an eye on it, and plant them in a little hill of earth. There comes up a plant with green leaves and white flowers, but the plant is of no value. After a few months you dig up the hills — I saw the natives dig them — and you find each hill full of batatas. What could be easier?'

'We will set you to growing them when we get back to Spain,' Magellan said, smiling.

Pigafetta began to tell what a good farmer he would make if he only had time to settle down. He would have chickens, geese, and ducks in a pond, two mouse-colored mules with scarlet harness and silver bells, a curly black spaniel for hunting birds, a cow that would give plenty of cream.

'No milk?' Magellan inquired.

'No, just cream,' Pigafetta said firmly. 'And a bull for fighting, also a fig tree, six orange trees, some grapevines, and a patch of batatas. Ah, what a dinner I will have cooked for you, Senhor Captain! And Juan shall serve it.'

Juan grinned broadly at this and walked proudly around the table with the steaming pudding.

Pigafetta smacked his lips and then burned his tongue on a large mouthful of pudding.

'Ah, I feel like a frog with a mouth full of red pepper! And look like one too, no doubt,' he said when he could speak.

Everyone laughed except Captain Mesquita, who was now pacing up and down the cabin.

'I think I will go back to my ship, Fernan,' he said to his cousin. 'It will soon be dark and I am not feeling well.'

The bay was still calm that evening, and they could hear the chunking of the oars as Mesquita's boat was rowed back to the Santo Antonio.

LATER a little wind came up. It blew loud enough so that no one heard Captain Quesada as he rowed from the Concepcion to the Santo Antonio. There were thirty armed men in the boat, among them Juan de Cartagena, once captain of the Santo Antonio, now a seaman in the Concepcion. Another of the dark figures, a fine tall man wrapped in a fine thick cloak, was Sebastian del Cano.

Del Cano's mind was full of pleasant thoughts as the boat crossed the dark bay. He had won money from Mendoza at cards that day and kept him from going to dinner on the Trinidad. Mendoza, a man who changed his mind easily, might have gone to Magellan's dinner if del Cano had not been there to play cards and to remind Mendoza of old affronts that he fancied he had received from Magellan.

Now, del Cano thought, our plans cannot fail. We are sure of Mendoza. Before many months Don Carlos will know that it was a mistake to pass over Sebastian del Cano.

To serve under the little lame Portuguese at all was bad enough, but not even to be captain of a ship ——

'Well, I shall have one soon enough now,' del Cano thought.

Now they were close to the Santo Antonio's side. There was no sound on her deck, but by the faint gleam of her lanterns they could see that there were dark figures standing there. The midnight watch, all traitors to their King, had come on deck and were waiting for the other traitors from the Concepcion.

It all went smoothly. No one, except their friends, knew when they came up over the side of the ship. No one heard them as they went softly to Captain Mesquita's cabin. The waves lapping against the side of the ship and the wind blow-

A lantern ... sent a pale light flickering across Quesada's cruel face, glinted on steel helmets, showed the irons on Mesquita's thin wrists. ...

ing against ropes and spars covered their sneaking foot steps.

They seized Mesquita while he slept and clamped irons on his wrists and ankles. A braver man might have struggled in silence. Mesquita cried out as the first iron touched his wrist. The master of the ship, Juan de Lorriaga, came running to see why there were screams at night from the Captain's cabin.

Mesquita always slept with a lantern burning. It swung from the ceiling and sent a pale light flickering across Quesada's cruel face, glinted on steel helmets, showed the irons on Mesquita's thin white wrists, shone on del Cano's handsome pink face and yellow curls.

Lorriaga was a brave man and a loyal one.

'If my captain is in irons, I am captain of this ship,' he said. 'I ask you, Captain Quesada, to take your men and go back to your own ship.'

Lorriaga was not long captain of the Santo Antonio.

They had their daggers out already. They stabbed at him fiercely and he fell bleeding.

'You are captain of the Santo Antonio now,' Quesada said to Sebastian del Cano.

'I am quite willing to accept the task,' said del Cano kindly.

Both captains then went out of the cabin, leaving Mesquita whimpering in his bunk and Lorriaga bleeding on the cabin floor. The plan had succeeded. Quesada's men had already seized the armory and overpowered the few loyal members of the crew.

Juan de Cartagena was sent back to act as captain of the Concepcion. Quesada stayed on the Santo Antonio. By the next morning he expected to be captain general of the fleet and captain of the Trinidad. On the Victoria Mendoza was only waiting for word from Quesada to rouse his men to mutiny.

It would be an easy matter now, Quesada thought, to overpower the little Santiago and the Trinidad and set sail — not for Seville but for Lisbon. There King Manuel would pay them the handsome rewards that Sebastian Alvarez had promised.

Quesada already saw himself receiving King Manuel's thanks. Alvarez had hinted that the King would give Quesada an estate and a title. 'Don Gaspar Quesada of — where?' He might name the estate Patagonia. That would do. 'Quesada of Patagonia.' There would, of course, be suitable rewards for Cartagena and Mendoza and del Cano. The Basque del Cano was a good navigator but in other ways a rather stupid young man. His stupidity was a good thing. Once put an idea in del Cano's head and only a knife would get it out, Quesada thought, with kindly scorn for the big Basque.

Even before they left Seville, Quesada knew, del Cano had felt that Don Carlos had slighted him. Mendoza and Cartagena and Quesada had played upon his feeling and told as many lies about Magellan as they considered necessary. Del Cano was now firmly convinced that he was doing a noble act in helping to punish Magellan for being a traitor to King Manuel. He did not consider himself a traitor. Certainly not.

It was a pleasure to Quesada to see del Cano getting the Santo Antonio's decks cleared for action.

Quesada could see no sign on the Trinidad that the watch there had noticed anything unusual about the other ships. If Magellan had heard anything of the mutiny, he gave no sign to the mutineers. Magellan was not a man who spoke before he was ready to act.

The next morning he sent a party of men from the Trinidad to get other men from the Santo Antonio and go ashore to fill their water casks. Vasco was in the Trinidad's boat rowing.

He heard the hail from the Santo Antonio's deck just as they reached her side.

The Trinidad's boatswain, Espinosa, answered that the Captain General had sent them to get a crew of men to help fill the water casks.

'Keep away!' bellowed del Cano's voice. 'No orders received here but Captain Quesada's.'

'Back water!' Espinosa ordered sharply.

The green water spurted and foamed back to the bow while the rowers turned their heads and gazed up at the grinning faces along the bulwarks above them.

'Swing around and go back to the Trinidad,' said the boatswain quietly, 'and put your backs into it.'

When they had crossed the bay to the Trinidad, Espinosa said to Vasco: 'On board with you, Coelho! Tell the Captain General what you heard. Ask if there are further orders for us or if we go on and get the water.'

Magellan received the news calmly.

Could he have known all the time that it was going to happen? Vasco wondered.

Magellan spoke as if he were carrying out a plan long made. He sent the boat first to the Concepcion and the Victoria to ask if they were for Magellan or Quesada. It was not necessary to ask Captain Serrano; he was known to be loyal. He had come back early that morning from his exploration down the coast.

The boat came back quickly with the news that the Concepcion and the Victoria were both for Quesada.

'Very well,' Magellan ordered. 'Go and fill your casks for the Trinidad and the Santiago. We have only two ships to water instead of five. Stay here, Coelho, Espinosa.'

Magellan limped up and down the deck in silence as the boat went off towards the shore. Vasco thought again of a lame black panther — most dangerous when quietest.

'There is a boat coming from our friends on the Santo Antonio,' Magellan said after a while. 'This becomes interesting.'

He welcomed Quesada's messenger politely and listened while he heard that Quesada was willing to make peace — on certain terms. This business about the short rations would have to be settled to the satisfaction of the crews. And there were other things to discuss.

'Captain Quesada invites you to come with us to the Santo Antonio and talk over these things,' the messenger said.

Magellan saw the trap. If Quesada got Magellan on board the Santo Antonio, there would be no need to discuss rations or anything else. The fleet would sail for Portugal with Magellan a prisoner.

There was nothing in his sea-green eyes to show that he saw this danger as he replied, with grave courtesy, that he thanked Captain Quesada, but that the Trinidad was the headquarters of the fleet. All business must be discussed there, he said.

'I am most willing to hear what Captain Quesada has to say. I await him here eagerly,' he added.

The boat went off with the message.

'Quick, Vasco. Tell Espinosa to launch a boat on the other side of the ship. Tell him to take eight men — fully armed — and to wait out of sight until these traitors come back with another invitation to come and be killed. You will stand where you can see Espinosa and me both. When the messenger comes on board again, wave your cap to Espinosa. He is to seize their boat and take the crew on board. Tell him to be quick and quiet about it. The boat is starting back here already and there is no one on deck over there — all below eating and drinking over their victory no doubt. Do you understand your orders?'

Vasco nodded and hurried off to Espinosa, then went back to where he could see Magellan. In a few moments Espinosa had his boat in the water on the starboard side of the ship. He rowed cautiously towards the bow and waited there. Vasco could see him from where he stood and he could see Magellan looking small and lonely as he waited. In a moment Quesada's messenger appeared again. Magellan was explaining to him in long sentences full of long words just why it was impossible to leave his ship for the meeting on the Santo Antonio. Before he had finished the first sentence, Vasco had waved his cap and Espinosa's boat shot off around the Trinidad's bow. There were shouts and curses from the Santo Antonio's boat, but the fight was soon over and Espinosa was bringing his prisoners aboard. One of his men towed the boat to the starboard side of the ship, where it was hidden from anyone who might come up on the Santo Antonio's deck. The messenger gave in tamely when he saw the other men in irons. It was all over quickly and without anyone from the Santo Antonio seeing what went on. Quesada, as Magellan had thought, was too busy drinking to notice that his boat was long in returning.

Magellan wasted no time. The short winter day was already fading. Darkness would help him.

'I would fire on the traitors,' he said to Gomez de Espinosa, 'but my business is to go to the Spice Islands, not to fight my own ships. Take only five men, Espinosa. Wear your cloaks. That will not look strange since the night is so bitter. Carry weapons beneath your cloaks. Take this paper to Captain Mendoza. It orders him to come at once to my ship. If he agrees, do not hurt him, but escort him here. If he refuses, do whatever is necessary to seize the Victoria.'

Then he turned to his brother-in-law, Duarte Barbosa, and said: 'You, Duarte, will take fifteen men, fully armed. Hide on the starboard side of the Trinidad until Vasco gives you the signal as he did just now to Espinosa. Watch his cap. Then row as fast as you can for the Victoria. Get aboard and help Espinosa to seize the ship. Hurt no one unless it is impossible to take the ship without violence.'

There was drinking on board the Victoria, too. Once the mutiny had taken place, there was no use saving the wine. There would be plenty for the journey back to Portugal.

Captain Mendoza was drinking at the cabin table. He started up unsteadily when Espinosa and his men appeared, and stood swaying while he read Magellan's letter under the light of the swinging lantern.

When he had read it, he laughed and threw himself into his chair.

'I'm not to be caught like that,' he said thickly. 'Quesada's captain of this fleet now.'

They were his last words. In the struggle that followed he

was stabbed. He was dead in a few minutes. Even before he died, Duarte Barbosa and his fifteen armed men had swarmed over the Victoria's side.

The crew of the Victoria were half-asleep and unarmed. Many of them had not been greatly in favor of mutiny. Some of them had seen mutineers hanged. Even a successful mutineer, they knew, could not go back to his own country. Besides, Mendoza with his lazy indifference when he was sober and his laughing cruelty when he was drunk was an unpopular captain. He had declared for Quesada without giving them a chance to decide for themselves on whose side they were. When they heard Mendoza was dead, they gave in to Barbosa without a struggle.

By this time Quesada had become uneasy about his boat. He staggered up on deck and peered through the twilight at the Trinidad. All was quiet there, but something moved on the Victoria near-by. Quesada rubbed his eyes. What he had seen moving was Magellan's own flag, with its bars of checked red and silver, being run up to the masthead. The icy wind from the South Pole snapped its folds and it billowed out against the last of the pale gold in the west.

'What shall we do now?' Quesada muttered to Sebastian del Cano.

Del Cano had no ideas. The two men gazed through the growing darkness for a while, first at the Victoria and then at the Trinidad. Then they went below to make plans.

But the plan Magellan had already made was being carried out.

As soon as he saw his flag, he ordered guns manned, decks cleared, arms served out. The Victoria and the Santiago were moving from their berths and anchored close to the Trinidad. All three ships were now between the mouth of the bay and the mutineers' ships. To escape, the Santo Antonio and the Concepcion must fight. Juan de Cartagena and Quesada and del Cano knew this without being told.

They knew, but they could not decide what to do.

'In the morning our heads will be clearer,' del Cano said wisely. 'Night brings counsel.'

'Yes,' said Quesada. 'We'll decide in the morning. Sleep now.'

In the darkest part of that night the decision was made for them.

NIGHTS—DARK AND BRIGHT ———— 14

THERE were no stars that night. The Antarctic wind brought occasional flurries of snow, which were white for a moment in the path of the Trinidad's lantern and then melted into the choppy sea. Sometimes a wave foamed white in the darkness. Vasco's eyes were getting used to the blackness now, and he could see that the Santo Antonio was blacker than the sky and the bay and the white frosted shore. He was perched in the bow of the Trinidad's smallest boat. Two men were rowing.

Vasco's fingers were cold from clutching the knife. Sometimes he could not tell whether he was still grasping it. Then he would touch the handle of it against his cheek. His teeth began to chatter.

'I am not afraid,' he said to himself. 'They just chatter because it's cold. I will think of hot things.'

He thought of red-damask curtains and plum pudding and Angela Luisa's red hair; of bringing the Princess hot soup in a silver bowl and of Maria de Sousa laughing at him in the light of a hundred wax candles, and of a red Irish puppy's silky ears. He thought of his mother's cloak of Russian sables and of his father feeding a red-and-green parrot in the sunshine...

Now they were close to the Santo Antonio's bow. He could hear Quesada above talking to the watchman.

'Just as I came on deck I thought I heard oars. It may be that our boat has come back at last,' Quesada said.

'No boat has come, Senhor Captain.'

Vasco smiled in the darkness and held the boat away from the ship's side. The deck boy must have been asleep, he thought. Quesada's footsteps went thudding away towards the stern.

Now they had slid along past the bow. Vasco grasped something slippery and cold as a snake and began to move the knife blade back and forth across it.

The rower behind him muttered, 'The cable, have you found it?'

'Yes, but I won't cut it through until he goes below. He won't stay on deck long. Listen and tell me when he goes,' Vasco said softly.

There came a screeching squall. The little boat rocked up and down in it. Somehow Vasco managed to hold the cable. He felt something warm running down his fingers. He must have cut himself when the cable was almost jerked out of his hand, he thought, but he went on sawing at the remaining strands of the thick rope.

The ship above him was quiet except for the wind blowing through her cordage. The blood was still running down his fingers. The cable was more slippery than ever. The rocking boat and the swaying ship above him made him dizzy. He kept on moving the knife, but every motion was an immense task. He began to see stars against the black waves where no stars were. The waves, stars and all began to beat in his head and he heard the man behind him say: 'He's gone below. Hurry!'

The last strand parted under his tired fingers. Like a horse who knows his halter has broken, the Santo Antonio leaped forward, jerking the cable from his hand. The knife clattered into the bottom of the boat and Vasco slumped after it.

'Row! Row hard!' he muttered, and slipped into darkness blacker than the darkness of a Patagonian night.

He had recovered his wits by the time they reached the Trinidad. He knew when they carried him up the ship's side. He felt someone wrap a cloak around him and heard Magellan's voice say, 'Well done, Vasco.' He heard many footsteps around him and knew that the men were loading the guns.

He opened his eyes. The only light was the gleam from the lantern on the poop, but it showed him men with cutlasses in their hands, others ready with grappling irons. His head cleared and he got to his feet. A moving lantern coming close now showed the Santo Antonio, carried by wind and tide, drifting down towards them. She was quieter than a cloud until she was almost on them.

Then there were shouts aboard her and Quesada's voice called: 'Man the helm. We're adrift!'

Feet pounded on her deck. It was too late for Quesada. Magellan's voice rang out and there was a burst of gunfire from the Trinidad, followed by the whistle of grappling irons. In a moment the ships were close together. The crew of the Trinidad were leaping aboard the Santo Antonio and from the other side men from the Victoria's boats were boarding her too.

Vasco saw Pigafetta, with a sword almost as tall as himself, come bounding along the deck. Vasco followed him, grasping his knife. He saw that his left hand was bandaged and wondered who had done it. He and Pigafetta jumped together across the bulwarks to the Santo Antonio.

As they did so a great shout went up from the attackers: 'On whose side are you? On whose side are you?'

It was Magellan shouting. They could hear him above the wind and the noise of fighting and the voices of his crew echoing him.

Pigafetta and Vasco ran towards Magellan. As they did so they heard the Santo Antonio's crew call out, 'We are sailors of Don Carlos, our King, and of Captain Ferdinand Magellan.' Vasco and Pigafetta were close behind Magellan when Quesada gave up his sword. Some of the men who had followed

Quesada the night before when he seized the Santo Antonio were now among those who yelled the loudest that they were for King Carlos and Magellan.

Quesada was put in irons and carried over to the Trinidad, while Magellan, who was as calm in victory as he had been in danger, gave orders for anchoring the Santo Antonio and the release of Captain Mesquita.

It took six men to put Sebastian del Cano in irons. Magellan did not speak as del Cano was dragged by him. Del Cano was silent, too. His yellow curls were tangled. One of his large blue eyes was bruised and half shut. His fine clothes were torn. Yet, as he glared angrily at Magellan, del Cano had a certain dignity. He did not begin to whimper that he was for Don Carlos and Magellan. Del Cano was ready to take his punishment. He and everyone in the fleet knew that it might be death. The King had given Magellan power of life and death over his crews. How this quiet man would use his power, no one knew.

The Trinidad's men were ordered back to their ship. Pigafetta climbed back over the bulwarks puffing loudly.

'Now, this was a very remarkable affair,' he told Vasco. 'How could the Captain General know just when the wind and tide would set the Santo Antonio drifting? Of course he can see in the dark, like a cat — but still it is strange how he knew at what time the ship's cable would part. Why are you not in bed, Vasco? Boys should be in bed at this hour, not out fighting. And you're all over blood — and bandaged. Don't tell me you've been stabbing someone? These things should be left to butchers. I am glad I did not have to use my sword, for to tell the truth it needs sharpening. It was my grandfather's. You ought to wash that blood — whosoever it is — off your face.'

'It's my own blood,' Vasco said. 'I cut my wrist. I suppose I rubbed some on my face.'

'H'm — let me see the cut. H'm. Nice clean gash. I will give you some of my secret ointment which I make by a rule of my grandmother's out of certain herbs. It is also good for baldness . . .'

The Concepcion was now the only ship hostile to Magellan. The other four ships were between her and the sea. The next morning an armed crew from the Trinidad demanded her surrender. Juan de Cartagena gave up his sword and was taken back to the Trinidad as a prisoner.

The mutiny had cost Mendoza his life. Juan de Lorriaga, a brave and loyal servant of the King, lay dying. Magellan might have executed all the leaders of the mutiny. He had the power. Their guilt was clear. However, he was merciful. Only Quesada, who had stabbed the dying Lorriaga, was executed. Cartagena was marooned on shore when, after the long, dark winter, the fleet again set sail.

Before they left Port St. Julian Serrano was made captain of the Concepcion. His own ship, the Santiago, had been lost on one of the exploring expeditions on which Serrano had been sent. Towards the middle of October there was a feeling of spring in the air and the fleet sailed south. It was some weeks afterwards that Pigafetta took up his pen once more to write about the voyage.

'On the Day of the Eleven Thousand Virgins, October twenty-first,' he wrote, 'we found, by a miracle, a strait which we entered by rounding a cape which our Captain named Cape Virgins. We sailed first into a great bay, like an inland sea. South of it were very great and high mountains covered with snow. The sailors said there was no way out of this bay, but our Captain said he knew well there was an opening and that it would lead into the Pacific Ocean. He sent the Santo Antonio and the Concepcion to discover the opening. The Victoria and the Trinidad waited. A storm came up and we were blown about the bay hither and thither.

'The Santo Antonio and the Concepcion were nearly wrecked by this same storm. They were driven to the end of the bay, where, expecting to be lost, they saw a small opening.

'They threw themselves into it and thus discovered the strait!

'It led into another bay. They went on still farther and found a third bay, bigger than the others. It was twenty miles wide and stretched away straight ahead to the south.

'By this time the ships had been gone two days. On the Trinidad we feared they had been lost in the storm, but suddenly a sailor who was on watch shouted. We all ran to the rail and there, coming from the south with all sails set and flags flying, came the Santo Antonio and the Concepcion. We knew what it meant when we saw the flags and the sailors began to cheer. To hail us the other ships shot off their guns and we, very joyous, saluted them with artillery and with shots. Afterwards, all together, giving thanks to God and the Virgin Mary, we went to seek farther on.

'About this time the Santo Antonio left us and sailed back to Spain, but without our knowing it. We wasted much time hunting for her. At last we left a message for her in an earthen pot, marked with a flag, and sailed on. We think that the pilot, Estevao Gomez, a man always opposed to our going to the Spice Islands, must have raised a mutiny against Captain Mesquita. This search for the Santo Antonio was a great trouble to us, as we had to search several arms of the strait without finding her.

'At last we sailed ahead and found the strait open right ahead of us to the northwest as far as we could see. We anchored near a river which we named the River of Sardines because we found a great quantity of them. From this place we sent a boat ahead, well supplied with provisions, to see where the strait led . . .'

The nights were growing long now. The day faded into a clear twilight that darkened so slowly that you could hardly tell when darkness came. Almost before you knew it was night the sky began to brighten again in the long twilight before dawn.

The boat — Vasco was in it — could travel both night and day. They took turns rowing. The strait was narrow here and there were many fingers of water reaching deep into the land. Yet they had no doubt about their course. Sometimes the strong ebb of the tide carried them easily westward, sometimes the flooding tide pushed them east and no matter how hard they rowed, they seemed only to crawl along. The water was always salt. There was no doubt that the strait led to the ocean.

The tide was ebbing that third night when it was Vasco's turn to row. There was almost no wind. The sun had left behind it a sky that faded from blue to amethyst and then to a darkness more purple than black. There were fewer stars in this southern sky than in the skies over Spain and Portugal. There were some brilliant ones that seemed to form a cross. For the first time that night Vasco noticed two misty patches of brightness that might be clouds of stars. The soft cool air, the snores of the sleepers, the regular beat of the oars, the foaming bubbles slipping past him, all made Vasco yawn and nod over his oar.

Still he rowed on, half-asleep, half-awake. Sometimes he did not know where he was. Sometimes he thought he was following Enrique through a dark street or watching Don Carlos draining a flagon of wine. Once he thought he was diving into green water. He saw Maria da Sousa in green and silver swimming towards him.

'Look out, Vasco!' she called. 'Look out, they'll catch you!'

'I'll catch you,' he said, and plunged after her . . .

There was water running down his face when he knew where he was again. The man in front of him, sleepy too, had caught the top of a small wave with his oar. The tide had turned. The dawn wind blowing against it was stirring up the surface of the strait into choppy white-capped waves. The waves tossed the boat a little but underneath them some deeper, stronger power was moving, a power too strong for tired arms to fight.

Vasco wiped the water out of his eyes and opened them.

The purple night was fading fast into the gray violet that comes before dawn. The starry clouds had vanished. Vasco looked for the shore. Then he rubbed his eyes again. Yes, the shore was still there, only no longer close at hand. It was far away, a darker, mistier gray than the water and stretching endlessly way into an ocean vaster than the sky.

For a moment he was alone with his discovery. The rowers, as sleepy as he had been, were tugging at their oars without looking around them. D'Espinosa, steering in the stern, watching for hidden rocks near-by, had not seen what lay in the distance.

Suddenly he looked up.

'Are you tired rowing, Coelho? It is your turn to rest,' he said kindly.

'We can all rest now, Senhor,' Vasco said. 'There lies the Pacific.'

It was true. The sun rose and gilded the sea around them and showed the dark cape reaching out into the endless ocean. Yes, this was the Pacific.

It was well named, Vasco thought, this peaceful ocean, this great pale silvery-green mirror for the sky. Even the dawn seemed gentler here than it did across the Atlantic, the tide calm in its great strength, the wind soft. The shores of the strait on the Atlantic end were starved and sullen. On the Pacific end there were green woods and fresh cool springs with celery growing around them. They had stopped and eaten it the day before and had broiled fish over a fire of fragrant cedarwood.

The last of the sleepers now woke up and immediately began to talk.

'The very fish,' said Pigafetta, who at once knew all about the Pacific, 'are cleverer than other fish. See, there goes a fish that flies like a swallow. Underneath, watching him, is a bonito. Now, the bonito knows well that the flying fish can fly only so long as his wings are wet. So the bonito watches for the shadow of the flying fish on the water. He swims along under the shadow. When the flying fish drops, why, there's the bonito's dinner. This is a thing marvellous and agreeable to see.'

'Just now I would rather see a broiled bonito,' Vasco said.

'In fact,' Pigafetta went on, paying no attention to Vasco, 'there is not in the world a more beautiful country, nor a better strait than this one.'

'What other straits have you seen?' Vasco asked.

'The Strait of Gibraltar, which is a very good strait, but nothing to this. Now, what,' Pigafetta said, changing the subject suddenly and skilfully, 'was the name our giant Paul gave us for the neck? I ask because a strait is a neck of water, and that reminds me that I have not written down some words of his language that our giant told us.'

'The neck in his language is schieleschin,' Vasco said.

'That is right, but you do not pronounce it enough in the throat, for that is the way our giants speak. He is a good giant — that Paul — and a good Christian.'

By this time they had turned and were rowing towards the waiting ships. The tide flowing strongly in from the Pacific carried them quickly, but it was many miles, so it was almost three days before they saw the ships again.

It was evening when they arrived again near the River of Sardines. The sun had gone down, leaving a sky full of great castles of pink cloud in the east and a fiery light in the west. In all this blaze of color the Trinidad looked small and dingy.

There was no one on her deck when they came alongside but Juan de Santandres. Juan was looking towards the shore. There was a party of sailors fishing between the ship and the shore. One of them was hauling in a fish and another was telling how big the one was that he had just lost. They were too busy fishing and Juan too busy watching them fish to notice the arrival of the other boat.

Vasco went quietly up the Trinidad's side with Pigafetta beside him. Even Pigafetta's footsteps did not disturb Juan.

He was too busy. Pigafetta crossed the deck and put his hands around the boy's neck.

Juan gulped out: 'Pirates! Help!' and began to kick.

'Not pirates,' Pigafetta said, 'but it might as well have been a dozen big-footed Patagonians. Where is the Captain General?'

'Writing in the cabin, Signor Antonio.'

'Go and tell him we have come — if you can leave your guard duty a minute.'

Magellan, however, had heard voices and was already limping towards them. He looked, Vasco thought, as if he had not slept since they left.

His voice was harsh and rough as he said, 'Your report, Signor Antonio.'

'Let Vasco Coelho — let the one who first saw it — speak,' said Pigafetta generously.

Vasco almost choked over the words, but they tumbled out somehow.

'The cape, Senhor Captain! We have found it — the cape you desired. It is there stretching far out into the sea. It's the Pacific, Senhor. Now we have only to cross it and find the Spice Islands.'

He had thought Magellan would smile, but the Captain's dark face did not lighten.

'He doesn't believe me,' Vasco thought.

Then he saw that Magellan was crying. This grim man, who had seemed made of iron through storm, cold, and mutiny, stood there with tears raining down his sunburned cheeks. He turned away for a moment, wiped his eyes on the back of his hand, then said quietly: 'I thank you, gentlemen. Since we have so long desired it, we will call that cape "Cape Deseado."'

They had passed Cape Desire now and the Pacific stretched before them. There were some who would have turned back, but it was too late. Before they left the strait, Magellan had consulted his officers. He felt that they were not speaking frankly to him, and late on one of those long light evenings, he sat down to write a letter to them.

'Perhaps,' he thought, 'they will understand me better if I write than if I speak.'

He twisted the quill first to one side, then to the other in his short brown fingers. Then he wrote:

I, Ferdinand Magellan, Knight of the Order of Saint James and Captain General of this fleet, which His Majesty sent for the discovery of spices, and of new lands in the Pacific Ocean:

I make known to you, Duarte Barbosa of the ship Victoria, and to the pilots and masters of that ship, that I understand that you think it unwise for us to go forward on this voyage. Now, I am a man who is willing to discuss plans openly, but it seems that after what happened in Port St. Julian — I mean the deaths of Luis de Mendoza and Gaspar de Quesada and the banishment of Juan de Cartagena — you are afraid to speak openly to me.

You ought to give me your counsel and I beg and command you to tell me in writing, each for himself, what you think about going forward or turning back. Do this, having no respect for anything but the truth.

When I have heard your opinions I will state mine, and give you my reasons for what I intend to do.

Written Wednesday, 21st November.

In 53 degrees of latitude, south.

In the year one thousand, five hundred and twenty.

When he had finished, he called Vasco.

'Make copies of this order of the day, please, and take them to the officers of the fleet.'

He stood watching as Vasco read over what Magellan had written.

'You are scowling, Vasco. Is the writing so bad?'

'No, Senhor, but I would not give the cowards a chance to turn back.'

'Do not worry,' Magellan said. 'I am only making sure that they put their cowardice in writing and sign it — or keep silent for the rest of the voyage. We are going forward, Vasco, even if we have to eat the leather off the masts.'

RATS AND LEATHER ———————

15

THEY sailed.

In six days they had passed Cape Desire. The Pacific stretched west, north, south around them like the pale silky rainbow-colored lining of a great shell. To the east the coast was only a dark line fading into a violet mist. They sailed north and the weather grew warmer. Soon after the first of the New Year they reached the Equator. They had turned west again by that time. It was as if the whole world were water.

The three ships seemed to crawl over this vast shining sea, as slowly as penguins crawl on ice. They thought of ice often now when the sun glared at them all day. One day was like another, only the water they drank became less and less like the clear water around them. It tasted bad and was a dirty yellow color. Yet it had to be measured by the spoonful. The biscuit they had brought from Spain was wormy.

Juan came up on deck one day with two pieces.

'See, Senhor Don Vasco' — he had settled down to this form of address and Vasco had finally given up trying to change it. 'See, choose your piece and I will race you with the other.'

'What sort of nonsense is this?' Pigafetta inquired.

'Not nonsense. You want to race, Signor Antonio? I get you a piece too. See — they walk!'

It was true: the pieces of biscuit moved slowly along the deck. This time, after Juan's biscuit had won a race of three inches, they threw the race horses into the sea.

Later they ate the biscuit, worms and all.

'After all,' Pigafetta explained to them, 'the worm has lived on biscuit all his life. He is only biscuit in another form.'

Unluckily the rats agreed with Pigafetta. Soon there was no biscuit except a few crumbs the rats had left.

Even Pigafetta began to grow thin.

'We remained three months and twenty days in the Pacific Ocean,' he wrote afterward, 'without taking in provisions.'

He described their troubles with the biscuit and the water, and then said to Vasco, 'It is strange that the Captain General should have said that to you about eating the leather off the masts.'

'Don't speak to me about leather,' Vasco said. 'I can hardly bear to look at my boots.'

'That is because you have a delicate stomach,' Pigafetta said. 'Now, with me it agreed perfectly well. Not that I would not have relished a good sauce with it — cheese, garlic, and red peppers, with perhaps just a few green olives sliced — but when crossing an ocean that no one has ever crossed before, you take what you can get.

'Let me see — where was I when you interrupted me?'

'You were just going to write down how I had to sleep in my boots because you kept hinting that they would be delicious with a little powdered sawdust,' Vasco suggested.

Juan giggled delightedly.

'Hush!' said Pigafetta with dignity. 'You disturb me.

'We also ate the oxhides that were under the main yard,' he wrote. 'They were put there so that the yard should not break the rigging. They were very hard on account of the sun, rain, and wind, so we left them soaking for four or five days in the sea. Then we cooked them a little on hot coals and thus we ate them. We also ate sawdust of wood and rats, which cost half a ducat each — when there were any.

'The worst misfortune was that the men's gums swelled and they could not eat these things. Nineteen of us died — among them Paul, our giant. I was sorry, for he was a most amiable person. Very few of us remained healthy. However thanks be to the Lord, I suffered no sickness.

'During these months we travelled four thousand leagues in this open sea, which is well called Pacific, for we met no storms. We saw no land except two small barren islands. There was no food nor water on them. We called them the Unfortunate Islands.

'If our Lord and His gracious Mother had not helped us with good weather and fair winds, we should have all died of hunger in that vast sea. I think that never again will man undertake such a voyage...'

While Pigafetta was writing, Juan de Santandres woke from an uneasy sleep. He had been ill and hungry many days now. Each day was like the last. He seemed to be living in a long, bad dream. At the end of it he had breathed in a delicious perfume. It was so real that he opened his eyes and turned his head. Vasco was sitting beside him. He was pouring something that looked like milk out of a hairy brown nut as big as a melon. It filled Vasco's silver cup.

He handed it to Juan, saying: 'Drink this. It will do you good. Slowly. Take small sips.'

'Is there more?' Juan asked after a while. 'Where am I?'

'Plenty. Hold the cup steady. This nut is called a coconut. At last we have found an island. You are on it, Juan. The coconuts grow on palms. Look up and you'll see.'

Juan soon grew better. The island where he was lying was called Samar. Magellan had had the sick men carried ashore. He had tents set up on the beach to shelter them from the blazing sun. It was hotter on land than at sea with a damp, heavy heat, but there was something about feeling the earth under them that did the sick men good.

Vasco and Pigafetta helped to take care of them, bathing them, bringing them fruit to eat and fresh water to drink.

keeping the insects away from them with fans made of palm leaves. Magellan, too, visited the sailors. Yet even when he was pouring coconut milk for them or arranging a screen of palm leaves to keep the sun out of their eyes, Vasco could see that the men were still afraid of him.

With Magellan nothing counted except his purpose. It was not that he was cruel. He was more merciful and just than most men. It was only that he would not bend or turn aside.

Vasco thought: 'He is like a magic arrow aimed for the Spice Islands. He pierces everything — clouds, storms, cold, heat ...'

Magellan was sitting alone under a palm tree gazing westward. He did not have to speak for Vasco to know that Magellan was thinking of the Spice Islands and of Francisco Serrano waiting for him there. This stay on the lonely island while the men grew strong must be hard for him, yet he had shown no sign of impatience as he limped about among them. He had even, at times, a smile that was almost gay. Yet the sailors did not like him. Vasco was probably the only one of the Trinidad's company who would have willingly gone near him.

Magellan turned at Vasco's footsteps. He had grown thin, Vasco saw. There were white hairs showing in his beard. His eyes looked larger than ever in his thin face. He had always looked as if he were seeing through and beyond the person to whom he was speaking. This look was now stronger than ever.

'The boy is better — the young Negro?' It was more like an order than a question.

'He will be quite well soon, Senhor,' Vasco said. He looked out to sea and added, 'There is a boat coming!'

Magellan said quietly, 'Yes, it has nine men in it.'

By this time some of the men in the tents had seen the boat, too. Those who were well jumped up and began snatching at swords and daggers and bows.

Magellan spoke in a voice, not loud, but so clear that it

could easily be heard across the beach. 'Stay where you are, men. Do not move, or speak without my orders,' he said.

There was a strange waiting silence while the boat splashed through the curling green water and touched the sand. Then they saw that the nine men were smiling and laughing. Five of them walked towards Magellan.

'He saw that they were sociable,' Pigafetta wrote, 'and he gave them some red caps, glasses, combs, and bells. When these people saw the politeness of the Captain, they gave him some fish, a jar of palm wine, some bananas, and two coconuts.

'These coconuts are from the most wonderful tree in the world. Now, we in our country eat bread, oil, wine, and vinegar, but they come from different plants. These people get them all from the palm tree. This is a marvellous thing.'

The visitors became very friendly with Magellan. The Malay Enrique could understand some of the things they said. Then Magellan knew that he could not be far from the Spice Islands. He took them aboard the Trinidad and showed them samples that he had brought of cloves, cinnamon, pepper, ginger, nutmeg, and mace. The men knew what spices were, and told Magellan — by signs — that they did not grow on this island, but on others not far away.

Partly to surprise the men, but more to show how pleased he was at the news, Magellan had the guns shot off. His visitors promptly jumped from the ship into the sea. However, they soon came on board again.

'When they went away,' Pigafetta wrote, 'they had very good manners and gratefulness and promised to come and see us again. There were many islands near the one where we first anchored, and our Captain called them the St. Lazarus Islands. Later the islands were called the Philippines...'

Juan was well again. Vasco took him out fishing in one of the ship's boats. It was lucky for Pigafetta that the fishers were near the Trinidad. Pigafetta was also fishing from the other side of the ship. It had rained that day and somehow — he never knew quite how — he slipped and went over the side into the water. No one heard the splash. Pigafetta spluttered and tried to call. He kept bobbing up and down like a cork in the water. He tried to call again, choked, coughed. No one heard him. He had kept his eyes tight shut all this time, but at last he opened them. There was a rope hanging over the side of the ship into the sea. He managed to splash towards it and caught it in his left hand. He clung to it and began to roar.

Vasco said to Juan: 'I hear shouts. Someone is in trouble. Let's go.'

'Don't hear anything,' said Juan, who had just pulled in his fourth fish, and was baiting his hook again.

'You wouldn't hear a lion that was going to eat you if you were fishing,' Vasco said, and began to row.

By the time they got to the port side of the ship Juan admitted that he heard something.

'Possibly a bull,' he said. 'Perhaps there is a bullfight in this sea. But no, it is only Signor Antonio bathing.'

Getting Pigafetta into the boat was almost as exciting as a bullfight. With his clothes soaked in water, he must have weighed two hundred pounds. The boat lurched and water came in with him. For a moment it seemed as if all three would be tipped back into the Pacific. Luckily the boat was a sturdy washtub sort of thing. It righted itself and the fishermen sat in it and laughed at each other. Juan's fish had managed to swim out of the boat when Pigafetta came in.

'I told you it was better fishing on this side of the ship,' Vasco said. 'The one I caught is the biggest of all.'

'It is not because of my merits that I was not drowned,' Pigafetta sputtered. 'I thank you, gentlemen. Unpleasant thing, drowning. So wet. I can't see how fish stand it. It was lucky I did not lose my notebook and also that I was not drowned, for otherwise who would see and report the mighty things of ocean? And especially now that there is something to write about besides water, of which, in my opinion, there is too much. Now, these islands are a good thing.'

'If you have an island,' said Vasco gravely, 'you have to have enough water to go around it.'

Pigafetta snorted at that and began to squeeze the water out of his hair. It was several days before he admitted he felt dry.

He found plenty to write about — or rather to make Vasco write about — in the next few days.

'It is my turn now to be waited on hand and foot. I am delicate. Very delicate,' Pigafetta said. 'Sit there and fan me, Juan. And Vasco, take some ink but do not spill any, for the sight of any liquid, except coconut milk, is unpleasant to me. It is not necessary to draw pictures of a fat man with a fish's tail, clinging to a rope, such as I found on a paper in my bed this morning. Today we turn to the literary art. Begin at the top of the page. Right there where it says, "This day the twenty-eighth of March ..." Now write what I say.

'Today we anchored near an island called Massava and soon saw a boat with eight men coming to our ship. The Malay Enrique spoke to them, but they rowed away looking frightened. Then the Captain showed them a red cap and some other things. He tied them up and put them on a little plank and pushed it towards them across the water.

'They snatched them up joyfully and went back to the shore. Two hours after two long boats came. Their King was sitting in one of them under an awning of mats. He spoke to Enrique and they understood each other well. The King would not come aboard, but he sent some of his men. The Captain entertained them well and gave them presents. They offered him a rather large bar of gold and a basketful of ginger. He thanked them but he did not accept these things.'

'Why do you think he would not accept the gold and the ginger?' Vasco asked.

'Our Captain is a man who understands how things should be done,' Pigafetta said. 'It is not fitting for him to snatch at the first lump of gold he sees as if we were pirates. He is the ambassador of a great king and must act as one ... Mend

your quill, because it makes a sputtering noise, which is very
bad for me in my delicate condition. It reminds me of water
... Thank you ... Where was I?'

'I think you'd got as far as Good Friday. That was the day
Enrique went on shore to say that we would like to buy food
for the ships and that we came as friends to these islands.'

'Right,' said Pigafetta. 'It was also the day the King of
Massava and his men came on board to bring us three china
dishes of rice for the Captain, and the Captain gave the King
that red-and-yellow Turkish robe.'

'He looked funny in it. He was so fat that it would hardly
meet around him,' Vasco said. 'How he jumped when we fired
the guns! I thought his eyebrows would meet his hair.'

'Were you there when the Captain had that soldier put on
steel armor and ordered three other soldiers to strike him with
knives and daggers?' Pigafetta asked.

'Yes, and I saw the men showing off their fencing and the
King opening his eyes and grinning when the swords clashed.
It was soon after the fencing that the Captain sent you ashore
with the King. I have not seen you since.'

'I will tell you about it and you can write it down,' Pigafetta said. 'When I landed, the King raised his hands to the
sky, so I did the same. Then we sat down and the King ordered a roast pig and some wine brought in. This is the way
they drink: First they raise both hands to heaven and then
take their drinking cups in their right hands and hold out
their left fists. When the King stuck out his fist at me — this
way' — Pigafetta balled up his hand into a fist and shook it at
Vasco — 'I thought he was going to hit me. However, I soon
saw it was a sign of friendship, so I did the same thing.

'Afterwards we went to the King's palace, which is built
high above the ground. We had to go up a ladder to get to it.
It was all covered with palm leaves. We sat on cane mats
with our legs doubled under us ... What do you find to laugh
at, Juan de Santandres? Nothing? Well, go on fanning me ...
They brought us a supper of fish and rice and freshly ground
ginger.

'Afterwards I slept on the cane mat I had been sitting on and some cushions stuffed with leaves. In the morning the King was very gay and kissed my hands when I went away. So I kissed his.

'The next day a brother of his, who is king of another island, came to the ship. He was the handsomest man we had seen in these islands. He had very black hair falling down to his shoulders from under a silk cloth and two rather large gold rings in his ears.

'He wore a cloth of cotton worked with silk from his waist to his knees and carried a dagger with a long handle of gold in a sheath of carved wood. He was scented with perfumes of that country. Each of his teeth was decorated with spots of gold so his mouth appeared full of it.'

'Must be a mighty fine sight, all those gold teeth,' Juan said.

'Continue fanning,' Pigafetta ordered. 'Vasco, take more ink.'

'You seem to think I swim in it,' Vasco said. 'I think I have written enough. Besides, it is time to eat. It is so sad that you are ill. We are having roast fowls with rice and ginger and grated coconut for dinner.'

'I feel better now,' Pigafetta said. 'In fact I am entirely recovered. Put down the fan, Juan, and tell the cook I prefer a wing, a slice of the breast, and plenty of giblets.'

Easter Sunday that year was very different from that cold, dreary day in Port St. Julian the year before. Magellan had never looked so happy as he did that day. Mutiny, starvation, and the vast Pacific were behind him. Only a little way off, he was sure now, lay the Spice Islands, the Moluccas, where his friend was waiting for him. There were sunshine, good food, and friendliness among these gay, laughing people with their shining dark eyes and gentle voices.

No European had ever seen these islands among which he now sailed, these Islands of St. Lazarus. Magellan had discovered them for Don Carlos. Soon now he would have found the road to the Spice Islands as well.

'It won't be long now,' Magellan thought, as he started for the shore to hear Mass.

Fifty men armed only with their swords and dressed in their finest clothes went with him. They were hot and sticky in their brocades and velvets, but the crimsons and purples, scarlets and blues were a gorgeous sight in the blazing sunshine.

Before Mass began, Magellan himself poured rose water on the hands of the two kings. Enrique had told him their names. They were called Rajah Siani and Rajah Calambu. Calambu was the handsome one with the gold teeth so much admired by Juan, who watched him enviously every time the King opened his mouth.

Both kings pleased Magellan by their willingness to take part in the Mass. They knelt beside him, kissed the cross when he did, raised their hands when he raised his. When the body of Our Lord was elevated, the ships fired off all their artillery and the kings knelt with the others and bowed their heads.

After Mass was over, there was swordplay by some of the crew and the kings watched it with pleasure. Later Magellan's men set up a cross to show that the island now belonged to the King of Spain. They all knelt in prayer at the foot of the cross — the kings in their cotton skirts and gold ornaments, Magellan in his Spanish suit of amethyst silk.

He had worn it at his wedding and once when he was knighted by Don Carlos. Beatriz had told him he looked splendid in it. With his limp and his grave face and his shortness, he could, he knew, never look splendid, but he was glad she thought so. If she could only be beside him today, how proud she would be, he thought, and how glad that she had always believed in him.

He wondered what she and his small son were doing. He was half the world away from them now, but the voyage

home, most of it in familiar waters, would go quickly. For a
moment he seemed to hear the bells ringing from every church
in Seville and see the quay lined with moving people. Beatriz
would be in front and Rodrigo would be in her arms waving.
Only of course Rodrigo would be too big for her to carry. He
would be standing beside her and shouting with the others.
He would be three years old ...

Sebastian del Cano, magnificent but steaming in crimson
brocade with fur on it, said to Magellan in his condescending
way: 'This is a very pleasant island, Senhor. These natives
seem like a very good sort of people. That fish they cook
with ginger is not bad at all.'

Del Cano was in good spirits that day. He found admiration
pleasing, and for the first time in his life he had all he wanted.
The natives were charmed with his fat pink face and yellow
curls and great height. There was always a group staring at
him with wonder and excitement. They brought him more
coconuts than he could have eaten in a month, cups of palm
wine, bowls of rice. They pointed to the sky and shook their
left fists at him. Some of the bravest of them even touched the
fur on the bottom of the doublet of this heavenly visitor.

To Vasco del Cano looked more like a hot boiled ham with
mustard sauce than anything else he could think of, but to the
natives he was gorgeously beautiful.

Ever since the mutiny del Cano had met Magellan either
with sulky anger or at best with indifference. It had now occurred to him that Magellan might, after all, turn out to be
important. There had been talk in Seville that Don Carlos
had promised that Magellan and his children after him would
be governors of the islands he discovered and receive part of
their revenues. There were evidently plenty of islands. It
would not be a bad thing to be governor of one. Perhaps he
himself might find himself governing these very agreeable and
admiring people.

'You did a very fine piece of navigation to get us here,' del
Cano said in his fine loud voice, a voice like the noise of beating

on a goatskin drum, Vasco thought. 'Yes, it was really remarkable.'

Magellan thanked him politely. On such a day as this, he could bear even del Cano.

'Of course,' del Cano added, 'if we had not sailed so far north after we left the strait, we should have reached here more quickly. A straight line is the shortest, I always say.'

Magellan flushed under his sunburn, but his voice was cool and steady as he asked: 'You knew they were here, then, these islands? If so, it was your duty to tell me so when we left the strait.'

'Well,' del Cano said, 'not these particular islands, but it was obvious that there must *be* islands, don't you see, because, after all, here is the sea peppered with them.' He laughed that loud laugh of his and went on. 'You understand the joke, Captain. We're looking for pepper and the place is peppered with islands. See?'

'I understand, thank you,' Magellan said.

Vasco, who was standing near, wondered why del Cano was not already in irons below deck, but del Cano was convinced he was being charming.

'It is a pity,' he boomed on, 'that the Trinidad does not sail so well as the Victoria. There's a trim little ship for you, Captain — ah — pardon, Captain General. I keep forgetting... Now if I had been in command, I should have sent the Victoria as straight as an eagle for these islands. It was a mistake to travel on the Equator, because, don't you see? — if this world is, just by way of example, a coconut, then to get around it, you have to go the farthest by the Equator. See?

'Now I promise you, Captain Magellan — that is, Captain General — that there'd have been none of this eating rats and sawdust if we'd followed my plan. Not that I mind a well-broiled rat myself...'

Del Cano boomed on, but Magellan had ceased to hear him. His thoughts had gone back to Serrano watching the sea from the shores of some island fragrant with spice. Suppose they sailed tomorrow. In a few weeks surely he would be looking into Serrano's kind blue eyes. Only he must not leave these islands here without making sure of them for Don Carlos. Even if by any bad chance Faleiro had been wrong, if Fate had after all set the Moluccas in the Portuguese half of the globe — still the voyage would be worth while if this other great and beautiful group of islands, which he had found, were added to the Empire of Spain. He — Magellan — was to be governor of whichever one he might choose. He must see others and make friends with more of these fat black-haired kings with gold in their ears and mouths. He must help them to become Christians. He must establish trade with them.

'These coconuts,' del Cano was saying, 'will be well liked in Europe. Take my word for it.'

Then Pigafetta and del Cano began to tell each other what they knew about coconuts, both talking at once.

Pigafetta had more speed, but, Vasco decided, in a long distance contest del Cano would win. And del Cano, Vasco thought, had more sense than people believed. He was conceited, but he was not a fool.

It was true that the Victoria was a better ship to handle than the Trinidad. Perhaps if del Cano had been alone in the Victoria, he really would have made the voyage in less time. He was strong as a bull, too. When the rest of the crew looked like living skeletons, del Cano was still pink and plump. He was as tough as that leather they ate off the yards.

'Toughness is what a man needs,' Magellan thought. 'On land the man is a tiresome blowhard, but at sea he's — well, he's a sailor. On my next voyage I'll make him a pilot. Perhaps even a captain.'

The swordplay and the eating were over now. Magellan left the island and went back to his ship. This island of the fat king, Rajah Siani's, was called Massava, Enrique said.

Enrique was proud and happy as they sailed among the islands, speaking his own tongue, teaching it to others, eating food he liked. He was respected by the islanders because he was the servant of the great Captain. The Spaniards and Portuguese respected him because he could speak with the island kings. Some of them, who had been in the habit of expressing their dislike of Magellan to Enrique by sneers and even occasional blows and kicks, now began to speak pleasantly to the Malay and offer him presents if he would help them in their trade with the natives. Enrique received these offers as he had the kicks, in silence.

He had nearly died during the voyage. He would have died if Magellan had not nursed him and fed him the last of his own preserved fruit. The Captain General himself ate leather and sawdust with the rest of the crew. Enrique did not know this until later.

'Is that true?' he asked Vasco.

'Yes, Enrique.'

'I tell you, Senhor Vasco. I never told this to anyone. I was a prince in my own place. The son of a rajah with better houses than these kings here. Now, I say that to be the slave of our Captain is better than to be a king. If it were not for him I would not stay on this ship. You know I could have gone away any day lately. They never would have found me in these islands. But to help my master I will even go back to Spain, that place where I scorched in summer and froze in winter instead of steaming comfortably all the year as human beings were meant to do.

'Now I will tell you the names of the new islands we shall soon see,' he added, and began to reel off the names: 'Seilani, Bohol, Canighan, Baibai, Satighan, Cebu.'

The brother of the King of Massava lived on Cebu. They reached it on Sunday, the seventh of April.

'Magellan went to Cebu,' Pigafetta wrote afterwards, 'because his fate led him there.'

It seemed a fortunate fate as they sailed into the harbor with the ships hung with flags. They fired their artillery and at first the people were frightened. Enrique explained that it was the way kings saluted each other — a sign of peace and friendship.

The King of Cebu tried to get the Spanish ships to pay tribute, but Enrique explained that the King of Spain did not pay tribute to anyone. They came in peace but there would be no tribute, he said proudly.

There was a Moorish merchant in Cebu who had seen the Portuguese in the Spice Islands.

'These people,' he said to the King, 'seem like the Portuguese. They are good friends if you treat them kindly, but if anyone treats them ill, it is the worse for him.'

'My master,' Enrique bragged, 'is the Captain of the King of Spain. He is far more powerful than the King of Portugal, both by land and by sea.'

'Does the King of Spain wish us to pay tribute?' asked the King of Cebu.

'No,' Enrique replied, 'only to trade freely and fairly.'

Pigafetta had a part in the talks that followed. He had been learning the language from Enrique. Pigafetta always learned any new tongue he heard — French, Spanish, Portuguese, Patagonian. He spoke them all very fast and inaccurately.

There were many visits between ship and shore in the next few days. Sometimes the men of Cebu squatted on carpets on the deck of the Trinidad while Magellan sat on a red-velvet chair and his officers sat on chairs of Spanish leather. Sometimes Magellan's men went ashore and carried presents to the King. They sat on mats with their legs doubled under them. Pigafetta surprised them by his ease and grace in this uncomfortable position. Vasco was hopelessly clumsy at it.

'That comes of being seven feet tall,' said Pigafetta.

Vasco said he was much shorter than that.

'You make the King's son look like a dwarf, and he is a fine tall man,' Pigafetta said. 'Now I must write about this prince.'

'The Captain gave the Prince some fine cloth,' Pigafetta wrote, 'and a quantity of glass, also a cup of gilt glass. Glasses are much prized in this country. Then he sent by me and another person to the King a robe of yellow and violet silk in the Turkish fashion, a red cap, very fine, and certain pieces of gilt glass. The Captain told us to put them all on a silver tray . . .'

It was Vasco who went with Pigafetta to carry the silver tray. It was heavy even for his strong arms. Enrique went too as an interpreter. They found the King of Cebu in his palace sitting on a palm mat. He was naked except for a cotton skirt, a cloth on his head, and his ornaments — a heavy gold chain and jewelled rings in his ears. He was a fat little man with a painted face. He was eating turtle eggs and drinking palm wine through a tube of cane.

Pigafetta noticed four girls who were playing on strange-looking instruments.

'Their manner of playing was rather musical,' he remarked.

Pigafetta himself was not musical, but on being asked by one of the young ladies to dance, he did so with enthusiasm. Vasco said afterwards it was like seeing a bear dance with a butterfly. However, Pigafetta's efforts seem to have pleased the King, for next morning Magellan received a message, delivered by Pigafetta, that a place was ready on shore where he could store his goods for trade.

The houses in Cebu, like those in Massava, were built high above the ground. Underneath were kept goats and hens and pigs. The young men of the place had a kind of bagpipe on which they played day and night. With goats bleating, pigs grunting, hens bragging about eggs they had laid, girls playing flutes and men playing pipes and drums, no one in Cebu was ever troubled by the quiet.

Trade began the next day and the Spaniards got gold for their iron and glass. The people of Cebu were fair traders. They used wooden scales like some Pigafetta had seen in France. Magellan, on his side, insisted on the sailors' giving fair value in exchange for gold. The trading was carried on in a friendly way for some days. At the end of the week, the King, to show his friendship, told Pigafetta that he would become a Christian.

Vasco was with Pigafetta and Enrique when they carried this message to Magellan.

'That day will be the greatest day of my life,' Magellan said.

SPEARS AND JAVELINS ———————

16

THE greatest day of Magellan's life was Sunday, the fourteenth of April, 1521.

All Saturday a noise of pounding echoed from the shore across the water. The natives were building a platform in the open air and shading it with palm branches. Magellan sent tapestries ashore to be hung up behind the place where he and the King would sit. He also sent two chairs, one covered with red velvet and one with violet.

He stayed on the Trinidad all day Saturday. Most of it he spent in prayer. Early on Sunday morning he went ashore. Forty unarmed men went with him. The only men in armor were two who carried the banner that Don Carlos had given him. It had never been unfolded since the day it was blessed in the church in Seville. Its velvet and silk and gold looked even more brilliant in the hot sunshine of Cebu than they had in the dim Spanish church.

Magellan took his seat in the violet chair after leading the King to the crimson one. The King sat on the edge of the chair with his short legs dangling and looking fat and uncomfortable. The platform had been covered with mats and scattered with cushions, so his followers were sitting at ease with their feet tucked under them. The Spaniards and Portuguese stood stiffly about in their fine clothes.

There was a long hot silence. Then Magellan rose and began to speak. Enrique stood near him, facing the King, and repeated in the King's language what Magellan said.

The King listened gravely while Magellan spoke about Christ and his life and about what it meant to be a servant of Christ. When Magellan stopped speaking, the King said that he and his people wished to be baptized as Christians.

Then Magellan took the King by the hand and they walked about the platform in great friendliness. Magellan said that the King of Cebu would be called Carlos after the King of Spain and that Ferdinand would be a good name for the Prince. The King of Spain's brother was named Ferdinand, he explained.

The priest baptized fifty men with names of Magellan's choosing. Afterwards they all heard Mass, and then Magellan went back to the Trinidad and had all the guns fired as a sign of joy.

'After dinner,' Pigafetta wrote later, 'our chaplain and some of us others went ashore to baptize the Queen. She came with forty of her ladies to the platform. We gave her a figure of Our Lady, finely carved, holding her little Child.

'As soon as she saw it, she wished to become a Christian, and the chaplain baptized her with the name of Joanna after the mother of the King of Spain. The Queen was young and handsome. She was dressed in white cotton printed with black. She had her mouth and nails very red and wore a large hat made of palm leaves. We gave her the carved figure before we went away. We baptized that day eight hundred natives — men, women, and children.

'In the next few days we baptized all the people of the island. Mass was said on shore every day. One day the Queen came in her state. Three damsels walked before her carrying three of her hats. She was veiled in silk striped with gold. After making a bow to the altar, she sat on a cushion and the Captain sprinkled her and her ladies with a perfume of musk and rose, which pleased them very much.

'The King and his brother also came and swore to be always faithful to the King of Spain. The Captain gave the King one of the velvet chairs and showed his servants how to carry it. The King then gave Magellan some jewels. There were two rather large gold rings for the ears and some for the arms and ankles. All were set with jewels.

'A brother of the King was very ill. He became well again after our chaplain had baptized him. This was a great miracle and when the people heard it they burned their idols, which are very ugly with large teeth like a wild boar's, turn-up feet, and painted faces.

'On Friday, the twenty-sixth of April, a man came from the island of Matan near-by. He brought a present to us from his chief and a message to say that another chief near-by called Silapulapu would not obey the King of Spain.

'The message said, "If the great Captain will send us a boat full of armed men tomorrow night, we will fight Silapulapu and destroy him."

'The Captain decided to go himself with three boats. We begged him not to go into this danger, but like a good shepherd he would not leave his flock.

'We set out from Cebu at midnight. There were sixty of us with armor and helmets. The King of Cebu and some of his chief men followed us in their boats. We reached Matan before daylight. The Captain tried gentle means first. He sent a man ashore to say that if Silapulapu would obey the King of Spain, we would be their friends, but otherwise they would feel how our lances wounded. The islanders replied that they had lances too. They asked us not to attack till dawn because they expected more men to help them. This was a trick to make us attack by night and fall into some ditches they had dug.

'We, however, waited for daylight. We then leaped into water above our knees. The water was so shallow that we could not go farther inshore in the boats. Our artillery could not shoot as far as the shore. We had to wade two good crossbow shots before we reached the beach. About a dozen men stayed in charge of the boats. The Captain divided the rest of us into two bands.

'When we got ashore, fifteen hundred islanders came down upon us with terrible shouts. We fired our bullets but they did not seem to stop them. They came closer, throwing javelins, spears, stones, even mud at us. They soon saw that while our bodies were protected, our legs could be wounded and they aimed their arrows and spears at them.

'Our Captain had his leg pierced by a poisoned arrow. He ordered us to retreat slowly, but most of our men ran back, leaving only six or eight of us with him. We retreated with him little by little, still fighting, and got out to about a crossbow shot from the boats with the water around our knees. The islanders followed. We fought them for an hour. They knew the Captain and aimed at him. Twice they knocked off his helmet. At last a native thrust a lance into his face.

'Our Captain struck back with his lance, then tried to draw his sword, but while he was trying to draw it a mob rushed at him. One of them had a great sword with which he gave the Captain a blow in his left leg. He fell and they ran him through with spears and lances...

'So they deprived of life our mirror, light, true comfort, guide...'

Of the six men still left around Magellan at the last, Vasco was one. He was wounded in several places, but he kept on fighting. His arrows and bullets had been gone a long time, but he still had his sword. The water washed around him, making his steps unsteady.

He and Pigafetta stayed by Magellan till the last. The last thing Vasco heard him say was a command to go back to the boats. The others went. Magellan kept looking back over his shoulder to see if they were safe and kept fighting to cover their retreat. He waved Vasco and Pigafetta back just before he fell. When they knew that he was dead, they started for the boats.

The men on the boats were shouting to Pigafetta to come on board or they would leave without him. The natives were already attacking the boats. On shore they were carrying off Magellan's dead body. Fainting from their wounds, Vasco and Pigafetta plunged through the water to the boats.

The King of Cebu would have joined in the fight but Magellan had ordered him to leave the fight to the Spaniards. The King wept bitterly over the news of Magellan's death. That afternoon he sent to Matan and offered a great ransom for Magellan's body. The answer was that no price would make them give up this sign of their great triumph.

Vasco knew little of the terrible days that followed Magellan's death. His arms and legs had been pierced by javelins and arrows. The wounds brought with them a fever that blotted out things. He remembered seeing Enrique, who was wounded too, lying near him wrapped up in his mat. Duarte Barbosa tried to make him get up and go ashore. Barbosa was the new captain. He had ordered the trade goods brought from Cebu to the ships. Enrique was needed as the interpreter.

At last, because Enrique still lay there, Barbosa roared that Enrique was still a slave even if Magellan was dead.

'You shall be returned to Dona Beatriz in Spain. In the meantime I'll have you flogged,' Barbosa shouted.

Enrique got up then. He looked pale and strange. There was a wound in his cheek.

He said as he passed Vasco, 'You know that the master promised that I would be free after his death, Senhor Vasco?'

'Yes,' Vasco said, and Enrique, after looking down at him for a moment said, 'Thank you. Good-bye, Senhor,' and went away.

Vasco never saw him again.

When his mind cleared, many days later, they told him what Enrique had done. Vasco could never believe entirely that Enrique had betrayed Barbosa and other men of the fleet into going ashore to a banquet with the King of Cebu.

Yet they had all been killed. Pigafetta's life had been saved only because he had been wounded by a poisoned arrow in the forehead and had stayed on the ship in great pain. Otherwise he would certainly have gone ashore, he said.

There were not enough men left now to work all the ships, so they landed on the island of Bohol and burned the Concepcion there, first carrying what they could use of her supplies to the Trinidad and the Victoria.

Vasco was still lying in a fever then, but Pigafetta went ashore at the different islands among which they were sailing. He would come back to the ship and squat down by the mattress on which Vasco was lying and tell what he had seen. Vasco liked Pigafetta's kind voice and his smile and the fruit he brought, but he was too ill to understand much of what Pigafetta said. It was a confused story of savages blowing poisoned arrows from pipes, of 'rather handsome' ladies, of porcelain vases hung on walls, of sugar cane, palm wine, and fighting cocks.

The king of an island called Borneo sent a boat to the ship one day. It was all ornamented with gold, and on the bow fluttered a blue-and-white flag with peacock's feathers above it. The men in the boat played on pipes and drums and cymbals. The music of the drums went on beating in Vasco's ears all day and into the night. He only half-heard Pigafetta's stories about riding an elephant through a strange city...

He was feeling stronger when he next saw Pigafetta.

'Tell me more about that elephant you rode,' he said.

No words could please Pigafetta better than 'Tell me more. He began at once.

'We went to the palace of the King of Borneo,' he said. 'We rode into a hall of it on our elephants. We walked then up a staircase and into a large room full of courtiers.'

'Like Spain?' Vasco asked.

'Not at all. We sat on a carpet. Our presents were placed near us in porcelain jars. At the end of this room was another. It was raised a little above the one where we sat and it was all hung with silk stuffs. There were two curtains of brocade caught up so that the windows could light the room.

'In it were three hundred men of the King's guard with naked daggers in their hands. At the end of it was an opening covered with brocade curtains. When these were raised we saw the King with a little child of his sitting at a table. They were chewing betel.'

'Is that the stuff they chew that makes their teeth red?' Vasco asked.

'Yes. Shall I tell more?'

'Tell me more.'

'One of the chief men told us that we could not speak to the King except in a certain way. This was it: I could speak to this man. He would tell what I said to one of higher rank. He would repeat it to the brother of the Governor, who was in the room with the soldiers. The Governor's brother would speak into a tube in the wall to a man who was near the King, and he would tell my thoughts to the King.

'This man then taught us to bow three times to the King with our hands joined above our heads, and then to kiss our hands to him. This was the greeting to royalty.'

'He could see you all the time?' Vasco asked.

'Certainly,' Pigafetta said, 'and hear us too, if he had wished to, I suppose. We told our message of friendship from Don Carlos, which was repeated through the tube, as I have explained. Then we offered our presents. The King nodded his head slightly when he received each one. They gave us some silks and some spices. Then we had a meal with thirty-two kinds of meat and fish. They were served with rice in china dishes. We ate with gold spoons like our spoons at home. The lights were candles of wax.'

'Tell me more.'

'Well, the city is all built on foundations in the water. When the tide is high women go through the city in boats selling food. The King is called a rajah. He's rather fat. No one ever speaks to him except through the tube, as I

have told you. They say he has two pearls as large as hen's
eggs, and so perfectly round that if placed on a smooth table
they cannot be made to stand still. I asked to see them, but
I do not know if the man who spoke into the tube repeated
what I had said. At least I did not see them. They have some
ships here called junks. The masts are of bamboo and the
sails of bark.'

'Are we still near that island?' Vasco asked. 'I should like
to see the King being spoken to through the tube.'

'We had to leave suddenly. Some junks started to attack
us and we went away. We are anchored now near Mindanao.
We stopped here to get news about the Spice Islands. It
seems we have been sailing in the wrong direction all the time
since we left Cebu.'

'Who is our pilot now?' Vasco asked.

'Juan Carvalho.'

'No wonder we sail in circles,' Vasco said sleepily. 'Did
we go to a place called Bataan? Enrique told me something
about it. I forget what he said. It is north and east of Cebu,
I think.'

'We are sailing south and west now.'

'Who is captain of the Victoria?'

'Sebastian del Cano,' Pigafetta said.

Vasco gave a low whistle. Pigafetta smiled. It was not
necessary for them to say to each other how strange it was
that one of the mutineers of Port St. Julian should now be the
Victoria's captain. It was — after all — only one of the
strange things: the Santo Antonio sneaking off while they were
in the strait, the sudden burst of recklessness that had led
Magellan to his death, Enrique's treachery, the murder of
the Spaniards by the Christian King of Cebu.

'He is a good captain. The men like him,' Pigafetta said.
'I have had some talk with him. He is less stupid than I
thought.'

'He fought well on the beach,' Vasco said.

At night when Vasco burned with fever, the whole thing

seemed like a dream. He expected to wake and learn that it
was not true that Magellan had died on the beach at Matan.
Matan. Bataan. These names echoed in his head like the
drums the natives beat at night. He remembered now what
Enrique had said about Bataan.

'They say my master is to choose an island of his own,'
Enrique had said. 'I have heard that there is a fine island
north of us — the best of all these islands. We should land
on a part of it called Bataan, they say. It might be hard to
hold that island, but a brave man might try . . .'

Vasco slipped back into the dream. Sebastian del Cano
walked stiffly through it, splendidly dressed, shaven, per-
fumed as he had been that first night in Lisbon, or eating a
broiled rat on the Victoria's deck and tossing the bones into
the Pacific, drinking palm wine with some dark-skinned king,
striding through water, sword in hand, and stopping poisoned
arrows with his shield.

However you saw del Cano he was always the same: handsome, calm, proud, and a little dull. It was hard to like him,
but hard not to admire him for his strength and courage.
And Magellan had said he was a good navigator.

Perhaps they would reach the Spice Islands after all.

SCENT OF SPICE —————————————— 17

AT LAST he was well again. The wounds had healed, leaving purple scars on his arms and legs.

'You have grown some more — another foot or so,' Pigafetta said. 'I get a stiff neck looking at you. You are taller than del Cano. That is, if you stood straight instead of bending like a piece of wet macaroni. Plain macaroni, no cheese, no meat sauce. Whose shirt is that you have on?'

'Mine.'

'Two of them put together would fit you well. You had better wear none at all. Get one of those cotton skirts the islanders wear, and some gold rings for your ears.'

'Good plan. Only would that cover my wrists?' Vasco inquired.

'Wear bracelets,' his friend advised, 'and be tattooed. With that beard you are growing you will look like the big hairy warriors I saw at Benain. They are very good archers and have swords as wide as your hand. When they kill their enemies, they eat the heart only with lemon juice or orange juice.'

'Orange juice for me,' Vasco said.

Pigafetta chuckled. He was in great spirits that day, because Vasco was well again. They leaned on the bulwarks together looking ahead into the blue distance.

Suddenly Vasco said: 'I see four rather high-rising islands in the east. I wonder what they are.'

Just then a Malay pilot they had brought with them pointed to the islands and began to talk fast and excitedly. They heard the word 'Moluccas.'

'He said they're the Moluccas!' Pigafetta shouted, and began bouncing up and down on the deck. Everyone came running and began to talk at once. Could it really be that these dark lumps on the horizon, not so very different from other islands they had seen rise out of the sea, were those Spice Islands they had sought so long? Yet it was so, and before long the wind brought them those spicy perfumes they had dreamed about.

'We gave thanks to God,' wrote Pigafetta, 'and to comfort ourselves we discharged all our artillery. It is not wonderful that we rejoiced so much, for we had spent nearly twenty-seven months, always in search of the Moluccas, and for many months we had been wandering among an immense number of islands.

'Friday, the eighth of November, 1521, three hours before sunset, we entered the port of an island called Tidore. Next day the King of that island came to the ships in his boat and we went in one of our boats to meet him to show him honor. He was sitting under a silk umbrella. In front of him was his son holding the royal sceptre. There were two men with gold pitchers to give him water for his hands and two others to pass him gold boxes of betel. His teeth were very red from chewing it.

'The King said he had dreamed that ships were coming to Tidore from a far country. He had looked at the moon and it had showed him that ours were the right ships. He came on board and we kissed his hand. We took him to the cabin, but as kings in that country do not stoop, he would not go in through the door. He went in feet foremost, from the deck instead.

'We made him sit down on our red-velvet chair and we

gave him a Turkish robe of yellow velvet. He gave us great promises of friendship and invited us to go ashore. Then we gave him the chair in which he sat, also linen, scarlet cloth, a brocade robe, three large mirrors, six scissors, six combs, some gilt goblets, and other things. We also gave presents to his son and to his chief men. When they went away, we fired all the cannon.

'This king is a man of a handsome presence. He wore a shirt of fine white stuff, the sleeves embroidered with gold, and a wrapper which came from his waist to the ground. He was barefooted. Around his head was a veil and a garland of flowers. His name is Rajah Manzor.

'He promised to give us cloves and to be a subject of Don Carlos. He told us there were five Spice Islands: Tidore, Tarenate, Mutier, Macchian, and Bachian...'

There had been war, the Spaniards learned, between Tidore and Tarenate. On the eleventh of November two boats from Tarenate came alongside the Trinidad. The first sign of their coming was the sound of drums echoing over the water.

Vasco heard it. He ran to the side of the ship and looked down into a boat. There was a Moor dressed in red velvet sitting in the stern.

A voice said in Portuguese: 'This is the son of the King of Tarenate. I who speak am Manuel, servant of Pedro de Lorosa, a Portuguese gentleman.'

There was a veiled woman in the boat. Beside her were two small children, a boy and a girl. They did not look like the native children they had seen among the islands. The first blue eyes that Vasco had seen among the islanders looked up at him from the boy's face, and the little girl had a fair skin and golden-brown hair.

'This lady,' Manuel said, 'is the widow of Francisco Serrano, a Portuguese gentleman. She is also the daughter of a Portuguese and of a lady of Tarenate. These are Serrano's children. They have come to find a friend of his called Ferdinand Magellan. Where is he?'

'He was our Captain,' Vasco said. 'He died in a battle on the island of Matan.'

Manuel spoke to the woman. She had already understood and had begun to cry and to wipe her eyes with her veil. The little girl started to cry too, but the boy stood up and said in strangely accented Portuguese, 'I will fight his enemies and those who killed my father.'

Manuel said: 'Be silent, Ferdinand. We are among enemies in this port. You promised, you remember, to be quiet if I would let you come.'

'How — how did Senhor Serrano die?' Vasco asked.

'There was a battle between Tarenate and Tidore. Serrano was Captain General for Tarenate. He fought so well that Tarenate won the battle. Peace was made, but peace is sometimes more dangerous than war. When Serrano visited Tidore some months ago, the King sent him some poisoned betel. He died in four days.'

The woman and the little girl cried again at this. The Prince of Tarenate looked at them impatiently. He seemed to take very little interest in the ships, but he accepted — with a rather disdainful air — a present of cloth, looking-glasses, scissors, and knives. When they went away, the little girl had stopped crying and was laughing at herself in one of the mirrors. The boy was stabbing the air with a knife.

The hot sunlight flashed from the blade into Vasco's eyes. He watched the boat sadly as it carried Serrano's family away.

'At least,' he thought, 'our Captain did not have the sorrow of knowing that his friend was dead. Perhaps they are together now where there is no treachery, no poison.'

The next day trade began in Tidore. The King had a building made ready for the Spanish goods, and the prices were agreed upon. Cloves were measured by the bahar — about four hundred pounds. For a bahar of cloves the Spaniards gave fifteen yards of red cloth, or fifteen hatchets, or

thirty-five glass goblets, or a hundred and fifty knives, or
fifty pairs of scissors. The King quickly got all their goblets
for himself. Many of the mirrors were cracked, but he took
them just the same.

Vasco's own trade goods — scissors, knives, and mirrors —
were soon gone. He had packed his mirrors carefully and few
were cracked. Soon there were Moorish faces reflected in
them and he had a good supply of cloves to pack away.

Manuel's master, Pedro de Lorosa, came to the Trinidad
one day and told them how King Manuel had sent Portuguese
ships to the Cape of Good Hope and also to Malacca to drive
Magellan's ships away from the Spice Islands. Since no Spanish ships had passed the Cape or Malacca, the Portuguese
were sure that they were all at the bottom of the ocean.

'King Manuel will be surprised,' Lorosa said.

'I hope so indeed,' Vasco said with a courteous bow.

Lorosa looked sharply at him and put his hand on his sword,
but after a moment thought better of it and went away.

After their cloves were safely in the ship, Vasco and Pigafetta went ashore. They wanted to see cloves growing.

'The tree from which they grow,' Pigafetta wrote, sitting
under one, 'is tall and thick as a man's body.'

'Some men's bodies,' Vasco suggested.

Pigafetta talked aloud as he wrote. It was not necessary
to look over his shoulder to know what he was saying.

'More or less, according to the age of the tree,' Pigafetta
continued.

'Or according to the thickness of the man,' Vasco added
helpfully.

'The bark,' Pigafetta continued busily writing, 'is of an
olive color. The leaves are like a laurel. The cloves grow at
the end of little branches in bunches of ten or twenty. They
are white at first, then red. When they dry, they are black.
Among these people each man has some trees. They pick the
fruit but do no other work around the trees.

'There is another island called Gilolo,' he wrote later. 'It is not far from Tidore. Nutmegs grow there. The trees are rather like our walnut trees, only with smaller leaves. The nutmeg is like a quince in shape and color, only smaller. It is downy like a quince too. Outside is a husk like that of our walnuts. Underneath is a thin red web called mace. Inside is the nutmeg itself.

'Ginger grows in Tidore. It is not a tree but a shrub. The leaves are good for nothing. The ginger is the root.

'After several days of trading, the King of Tidore invited us to a feast. We heard that Serrano, a friend of our dead Captain's, had been killed by the natives, so we began to suspect treachery. We remembered the unfortunate feast given to our men on Cebu, and we decided on a speedy departure.

'The King was grieved and made good speeches about his friendship for Spain. A great many cloves were brought to the trading place in the next few days and we began to buy cloves like mad. Towards the end of the time the natives would give us a bahar of cloves for a yard of ribbon ...'

At last the ships were so heavy that they could hold no more. On the fifteenth of December they bent on the new sails that Magellan had provided for the voyage home. Painted on them was the cross of Saint James and letters which said, 'This is the figure of our good fortune.'

There were boats full of islanders in the harbor staring at the new sails. One of them moved to the sound of cymbals and there were streamers on it of red, white, and yellow parrot's feathers. The air was full of the scent of cloves.

The King of Tidore sent aboard presents for the King of Spain. Among them were two birds of paradise with their soft plumes of feathers.

The Spaniards were hauling up the Trinidad's anchor when it was found that she was leaking badly. The men worked all day at the pumps, but the water only came in faster. The King ordered his divers to go down under the sea and find the leak. These men went down with their long hair loose, thinking it might be sucked into the leak and show where it was, but though they stayed under water for half an hour they could not find the hole.

The Monsoon that would send them home had already begun to blow. They decided to leave the Trinidad to be repaired and for the Victoria to start at once. Vasco watched the Victoria getting ready to leave with a heavy feeling in his throat. Homesickness swept over him so strongly that the Spice Islands with their strange trees and houses, their parrots, palms, and sugar cane, their gaily decorated boats and jewelled Kings, seemed like some ugly and terrible poison.

The King of Tidore had told them never to leave their ships at night because there were men who walked about his city without their heads.

'They carry a certain ointment,' he had said. 'If they wish to make anyone ill, they touch his palm with it and he dies within three days. They can make people dizzy without touching them. I keep watch for them and have a few executed every now and then.'

Vasco felt as if some headless man had touched his palm with that ointment. He stared down into the oily green water hardly noticing the boat crossing from the Victoria to the Trinidad with Sebastian del Cano sitting in the stern.

Del Cano was the Victoria's captain now. He walked stiffly across the deck to where Vasco and Pigafetta were standing.

'I understand you wish to return with me, Signor Antonio,' he said to Pigafetta.

'If there is room, Captain,' Pigafetta said.

'Two of my men wish to stay and sail with the Trinidad. She will sail for Yucatan when the west wind blows. By then she will be ready for the sea again. I can take two men,' he said in his loud, slow voice.

There was a pause and Vasco heard his heart beating.

'I believe you have some skill with charts, Coelho,' del Cano said. 'How many cloves did you have?'

Vasco told him in a voice that sounded strange in his own ears.

'About the same as Gines di Mafra. You could make some arrangement with him. He wishes to sail on the Trinidad. It is only fair to tell you that many of the men feel that the Trinidad's voyage is the safer one. We have shoals ahead of us, the Cape of Storms to double, Portuguese ships may attack us. The Trinidad will sail to Darien on the Isthmus of Panama. The crew will land and find another ship to take them to Spain. They may well reach there ahead of us. Take your choice, Coelho. Sail east or west?'

'May I take Juan de Santandres with me? I promised him to take him home as my servant.'

'The little African who sings with the loud voice? Yes, if he likes to act as deck boy.'

'Then I will sail west. And I thank you, Captain,' Vasco said.

'There is no need of thanks. You will work your passage,' del Cano said in his stiff way.

Suddenly Vasco realized that del Cano was looking up at him. The Captain was a mere six feet in height. Vasco topped him by three inches. All at once Vasgo forgot about that magic ointment on his palm. Probably the King had executed all the headless men, a few at a time. Only how did you execute a man who walked around carrying his head in his hand? Well, he would never know now.

Suddenly he felt wonderful. The strange feeling in his throat had gone.

'Nevertheless, I thank you, Senhor Captain,' he said smiling.

CAPE OF STORMS ———————————— 18

ON THE twenty-first of December the Victoria sailed from Tidore. She waited till midday while the men on the Trinidad wrote letters home to Spain. At noon both ships fired their cannon in farewell. By evening the pointed mountains of the Spice Islands had begun to fade in the distance.

Two pilots from Tidore showed them the way among the new islands they passed. They also told them many interesting things about the people who lived there. Pigafetta wrote these things down. There was a story that some of the people had ears so long that they lay down on one and wrapped the other around them. It was disappointing when they looked eagerly at the people in every harbor to find that they had ears like anyone else with gold rings in them. The pilot also told them about large birds that carry off elephants, but they did not see any of them either. Apparently they did not find the right island.

The pilots told them stories about Java as they sailed past it and also about Siam and Cambodia and China. The stories grew more remarkable the farther away the place was. Vasco liked one about a Chinese king who rode on a peacock with his wives into the mouth of a snake. The snake had, conveniently, a glass window in his breast. You could look through and see the King, but you could not tell him from his wives.

These stories made places they passed through such as Calicut and Sumatra seem rather dull. Most of the people seemed to live by fishing and growing things, and, except for wearing fewer clothes than people in Lisbon or Seville, seemed to live no more exciting lives than people in those cities.

The Victoria made a good crossing of the Indian Ocean, yet by the time they reached the coast of Africa many of the crew were ill. They had only rice to eat. All their meat had spoiled because they had not been able to salt it. The ship began to leak and many of the crew begged del Cano to stop at Mozambique. This was a Portuguese colony, and del Cano did not stop for fear of being captured by the Portuguese.

'Prizing honor more than life, we decided at all costs to return to Spain,' Pigafetta wrote. 'We suffered greatly from cold after that. In order to double the Cape of Good Hope we went as far south as latitude 42°. We remained off that cape for nine weeks with our sails struck, because of the fierce western gales that beat against our bows. At length by the aid of God, on the sixth of May, 1522, we passed that terrible cape . . .'

It was one of those icy nights when the Victoria with bare masts was taking the buffetings of a western gale that howled out of the ocean sea around the Cape of Good Hope. It was Vasco's watch on deck. They were shorthanded. More of the sailors had fallen ill with scurvy. Juan was one of them, and Vasco was doing his work, watching the sand in the hourglass, turning the glass when the sand had run through, calling out the hours — one so like the last in the dark and cold. Spray blown off the top of some frothing billow spattered him from time to time. The ship creaked as she pitched and the light in the lantern flickered.

The wind bit through his sailor's coat. It was too small for him. His wrists stuck far out of the sleeves and it would no longer fasten across his chest. Sometimes he blew on his cold

fingers to warm them; sometimes he slapped his arms across
his chest; sometimes he sang.

It was months ago since he had last sung this song. Then
his voice had still cracked at times. Now he felt as if he could
howl the wind down, but he sang softly — or thought he did —
the song he had made for Tonio in the inn at Valladolid.

'I will see if the world is round,' he began, and sang it all
through. Then he added a new verse.

> 'Where the cross hangs in the sky
> And the Cape says, "Round me? Never!"
> I will sail where the wind blows high
> Forever.'

'This is the kind of song that goes on forever,' he thought.
'Let me see — are there any more rhymes?'

> 'Now I know the world is round,
> I have seen it, sky and billow,
> And from east to west I've found
> My pillow.
>
> Where he lies, they beat the drums
> Ever louder, ever faster.
> I'll be waiting till he comes —
> My master.'

He sang it over again, not so loud as the wind, more softly
than the tune that he would sing when he turned the glass
over. He kept time to his singing with his feet, to warm them.

When he finished a voice behind him said, 'You find this a
good night for singing, Coelho?'

Vasco turned and saw del Cano's face in the flickering
lantern light. Even in this gale the Captain still looked like
a handsome wooden statue, but his voice was less cold than
usual.

'I keep myself warm, Senhor Captain,' Vasco said. 'I sing
for cheerfulness.'

"The tune was sad, I thought, but you Portuguese are like
that, I remember. The sadder the song, the better you feel ...
The wind still blows from the west, I see. I dreamed it had

He sang it over again, not so loud as the wind, more softly than the tune that he would sing when he turned the glass over.

shifted and came on deck. I'll go below,' del Cano said, but he still stood there with salt spray trickling down his fine straight nose.

Vasco looked back at his glass. The sand had almost run out.

'Sometimes,' del Cano said, 'I think we shall never double this cape. More than eight weeks of this! We may starve or go to the bottom before this stubborn wind shifts. I wonder what he would have done.'

'Who, Senhor Captain?'

'Your master, about whom you still sing as if he were alive, though he lies dead under the palms, or burned to ashes in front of some pig-faced idol. That great navigator whom I was too stupid to understand — until too late.'

For a moment del Cano's voice seemed to Vasco unreal, like something half-heard in the roar of the wind, but the Captain was there beside him, solid and stiff as ever.

After a pause del Cano spoke again.

'Did he ever tell you anything about this cape?'

'He said that once he ran close in shore to double it,' Vasco said, 'in spite of the danger.'

'He was at his best in danger,' del Cano said, 'and saved others from it. Do you remember how he waved us back in the fight? How he kept the savages off us while we were retreating?'

'Yes,' Vasco said. 'I remember.'

'It would be bad to think of at night if you were like me and had fought against him at St. Julian. And if he had forgiven you and sent you back to your ship. You are lucky, Coelho. You were always faithful to him. Pigafetta says his men did not love him. It is true that he had a stern way that made it hard to like him. But you knew him better, I think.'

'Yes,' Vasco said. 'I knew him . . . The sand has run out, Senhor Captain. It is time for the call.'

He turned the glass, struck the bell, and sang out: 'One

hour passed in two turns and more will pass if God will. Let us pray God to grant us a good voyage and to the Mother of God, who is our guide, to deliver us from pumping out water and other troubles. Forward, ahoy!'

It was Magellan who had taught him the call. As he listened for the voice of the watch on the forecastle, Vasco felt for a moment as if Magellan were standing beside him. But it was del Cano who spoke.

'I'll run inshore tomorrow,' he said abruptly as Vasco finished singing, and walked off into the darkness.

The next morning he was as cool and stiff as ever. Vasco would have thought he had dreamed their talk of the night before except for one thing.

They were running in close to the cape.

They doubled it the next day.

A strange thought came to him. Magellan and del Cano were alike in one way: they were both at their best in danger — better than their best, perhaps. It was almost as if Magellan had spoken to del Cano across those dark waters.

'We then sailed northwest for two whole months,' Pigafetta wrote. 'Twenty-one of the crew died in that short time, both Spaniards and the men who had sailed with us from the Spice Islands.

'Being very short of food we touched at the Cape Verde Islands on Wednesday, the ninth of July. There we bought two boatloads of rice. The men who went ashore asked what day it was. They were told it was Thursday, which was a cause of wonder, because with us it was Wednesday. I was more surprised than anyone, because I had kept my diary every day, always noting down the name of each day.

'Afterwards it occurred to me that, as we had always sailed west, following the sun, we must have gained a day. This is clear to anyone who thinks about it.

'One of our sailors foolishly offered to pay for some rice with cloves. The Portuguese thus learned who we were and seized our boat and thirteen men. They would have taken our ship too, but we escaped.

'It is now, as I am writing this, the sixth day of September and we shall soon enter the Bay of San Lucar. There are only eighteen of us now, and most of us are sick. Some have died of hunger. Some were buried at sea. I reckon that we have travelled more than fourteen thousand leagues and have gone around the world from east to west.

'I have no gold and silver to present to His Majesty Don Carlos, but I have this book of mine telling what happened on our voyage, which will be more precious, I hope, in the eyes of so great a sovereign,' Pigafetta wrote with his usual modesty.

In telling the King about Magellan's death, Pigafetta had this to say: 'He died; but I hope that Your Illustrious Highness will not allow his memory to be lost, so much the more since I see also in you the virtues of our great Captain, for one of his chief virtues was constancy in ill fortune. In the midst of the sea he was able to endure hunger better than we. Most versed in nautical charts, he knew better than others the true art of navigation. Of this it is certain proof that by his own genius and courage, without anyone's giving him an example, he so nearly completed the circuit of the globe.'

It took two days to sail from San Lucar to Seville. On the eighth of September, 1522, they cast anchor near the quay from which they had sailed and fired off all their artillery.

The next day they went barefoot, wearing their shirts, with candles in their hands, to the Shrine of Santa Maria of Victoria to give thanks for their safe return.

In all the crowds of curious people that followed them to the church, there was no face that Vasco had ever seen before. Not even in the harbor of Tidore had he ever felt more lonely than in this church where he had often prayed.

The streets seemed strange to him. The gray houses shut out the sunshine and shut in heavy air that held no scent of cloves and nutmeg. He began to long for airy wooden houses, stuck up on stilts with cocks and pigs underneath them. He missed thumping drums, squealing bagpipes, smiling people bringing china dishes of roast pig and rice and ginger.

Here in Seville people looked at him gravely but curiously as if he were a native from some strange land.

'They look,' he said to Pigafetta, 'as if they thought I was walking around with my head under my arm getting ready to touch their palms with magic ointment. For half a bahar of cloves I'd take six of them and knock their heads together.'

'I think you had better shove off and go back to the ship,' Pigafetta said in some alarm. 'It is just possible that you — we — look different from these natives here.'

'What's the matter?' Vasco asked. 'I've got on a shirt, haven't I? I'm not wrapped up in one of my ears or walking around in a snake's stomach.'

'True, but the inhabitants of Seville seem to wear shoes and jerkins. Also — forgive me — isn't that a cotton skirt from Cebu that you are wearing?'

'No one on the ship had any breeches big enough for me,' Vasco explained.

'I think tomorrow you had better sell your cloves, and then visit a tailor. I cannot advise you to visit Don Carlos in that skirt. It is well, in Spain, not to look too remarkable.'

Vasco did indeed look a little too remarkable for the streets of Seville, especially when walking with Pigafetta. The plump little knight was nearly two feet shorter than Vasco, who had grown another inch or two on the voyage. Vasco was burned the color of an old pigskin saddle. In one of the islands — he had taken Pigafetta's advice — his skin had been tattooed with various pictures. The children who were following him were charmed with the Victoria under full sail on his chest. His shirt was unfastened and showed most of it. They also liked the snakes on his right wrist. It was a pity they could not see his back, on which a large bird was flying away with a rather small elephant.

Vasco had gold rings in his ears, and around his neck a

heavy gold chain with a gold locket hanging from it. With his wild mop of curly brown hair sticking out from under a piece of gold-embroidered silk, his curly brown beard that had never been cut, the fading purple scars on his legs and among the tattooing on his arms, his skirt of printed black and white cotton, his Malay sword in its carved wooden sheath at his side, it is no wonder that the children were at his heels. He was a walking geography lesson. Several of the boys who were following decided to run away to sea at the first opportunity. Two of them did later and were found and sent home, and ate their meals standing up for several days.

'If you take such long steps,' Pigafetta panted, 'I shall have to run, which is undignified. You forget that I am a Knight of Rhodes and a famous writer. At least I shall be famous if you do not cause me to die from shortness of breath before I present my book to Don Carlos.'

'I will carry you with one hand, my famous little fat author,' Vasco said kindly.

'I thank you — no. I still have my own legs, the same ones I set out with. Mine haven't grown two feet,' Pigafetta said.

They came in sight of the river and the quay. How shabby and small the Victoria looked as she lay there among the fine new ships with their gilded carving and new paint and clean sails! Yet it was the Victoria — the small, brown wild duck among swans — at which the people along the riverbank were pointing.

'That,' Vasco heard a man say to his little boy, 'is one of the giants they brought home. Patagonians they call them. This I learned from a member of the crew of the Santo Antonio, which came home from the Strait of Magellan instead of sailing around the world. The crew are all in jail waiting to be tried for mutiny against Captain Mesquita and deserting the fleet. I have talked with this man from the Santo Antonio through the bars... See what large feet the Patagonian has, my son! He looks fierce, but I hear they can be tamed and are gentle if kindly treated.'

Vasco looked around for the Patagonian. Then he saw that Pigafetta was doubled up laughing with tears running out of his green eyes. Vasco realized that he himself was the Patagonian and began to laugh too. The small boy was frightened and his father carried him off, telling him that he wouldn't let the giant hurt him.

Vasco was glad to hear that the crew of the Santo Antonio were in jail. They certainly deserved to be there. He was glad, too, to get away from the staring crowd and back on board the Victoria. The ship was cramped and dingy. Every inch of it smelled of cloves. Perhaps it was the smell of spice that made it seem like home. He felt comfortable in the stuffy little cabin where he could not stand up straight. One of the violet velvet chairs was still there. It was the one on which Magellan had sat on the platform at Cebu on the day of his great happiness. The velvet was beginning to look shabby. Del Cano had often thrown himself down on it when his clothes were wet with salt spray from the gales around the Cape of Good Hope.

He was sitting in it now with his elbows on the table and his chin in his fists. He was scowling down at a paper with words scrawled on it and scratched out — mostly scratched out. The pen was pushed back of his ear. The feather stuck out from among his yellow curls.

Del Cano writing — or trying to write — was something new.

'Don Carlos has sent for me,' he announced. 'I am writing my report.'

Pigafetta gave a little chuckle.

'And sweating over it,' he remarked. 'People think writing is a lazy habit. To me it is a pleasant sight to see the man who weathered the gales of the Cape of Storms for nine weeks sitting here steaming over pen and paper. May a fellow writer glance at your account? . . . H'm . . . "Friday, 9th December, took sun 88' . . . Bay St. Lucy, 7 fathoms, foul bottom . . . Item, Sunday, 12th . . . did not take sun, but ran S.W. and a quarter" . . . And this goes on for three pages!'

'Of course,' del Cano said, 'it's a little dull.'

'A little dull!' exclaimed Pigafetta. 'My dear fellow, you are unfair to yourself. Why, this is without exception the very dullest thing I ever read. Your gracious King — and he's an emperor now too, I hear, by the way — will split himself yawning within three minutes.'

'Perhaps,' del Cano suggested flushing, 'you would like to write it yourself.'

'Certainly. That is, I will pace up and down, for I think best on my feet, and this Patagonian giant I have tamed shall write down what I say. Furthermore, we will go to Court with you when you read it. To give you confidence.'

Del Cano glanced at Vasco's costume.

'Vasco Coelho plans to visit the tailor tomorrow, as soon as he sells his cloves,' Pigafetta said soothingly. 'He will be dressed in a style more — well, more Spanish. Sit down, Vasco. Take some ink, and begin thus:

'We come to report to your Imperial Majesty a voyage such as was never before made in the history of this world . . .'

('Take more ink.')

IT WAS strange, Vasco thought, that life in Spain had changed so little. Here was Don Carlos again in a fine, airy room hung with splendid tapestries, eating his dinner in his neat way, looking scarcely older than when Vasco had seen him last. He was an old-looking young man and would probably be a young-looking old one.

As usual, after dinner, the pages carried away the table and the silver jugs and dishes and set his chair near a window. It was a fine chair covered with crimson velvet, much like the one Magellan gave to the King of Cebu.

People began to go up to Don Carlos and speak to him. Nothing had changed. Vasco was glad of that. He heard the voice of a man asking the King some favor and he thought of the King of Borneo and his speaking-tube. A mile of speaking-tubes would not make a great king. Don Carlos was great enough to meet men face to face.

Del Cano got through his speech well in his wooden style. Vasco could see that Pigafetta was twitching with impatience to tell the news with the flourish it deserved. To hear del Cano you would think he had done nothing more exciting than walk down to the wharf and buy some sardines for supper.

Vasco and some of the other members of the crew had carried in the things that had come from the islands — the coconuts, the preserved ginger, the jars of misty green porcelain the color of a cool sea under fog. There were blue and

white jars too, like the sky in a northwest breeze. There were
the stuffed birds of paradise, and pieces of embroidered cotton, cloth made of bark, shells from distant beaches, a little
heap of pearls. Juan carried a gold box of betel nut and one
of cloves. Vasco had a porcelain dish full of gold and jewelled
ornaments.

While these things were being presented to the King, the
Malay sailors stood as if they had been carved out of brown
wood. Don Carlos spoke to them and Pigafetta translated
what he said into their language. In speaking any language
Pigafetta always made up for any gaps in his knowledge by
using his hands, shoulders, elbows, and eyebrows. People
generally understood him — giant Patagonians, Malay traders, a king at the end of a speaking-tube, rather handsome
ladies with straw hats, Portuguese pirates, and this serious
young man whose titles covered a page of a large book.

Pigafetta translated what the Malays said into French
with a strong Italian accent and King Charles replied in
Spanish flavored with French and Dutch. Everyone understood everyone else except possibly del Cano, whose blue eyes
grew just a little more prominent than usual.

It was bad enough, del Cano thought, never to hear anyone
speaking properly as Basques speak, to have to sail for years
with Spaniards and Portuguese, without having to listen to
all the tongues in the Holy Roman Empire mixed together.

However, he had understood Don Carlos when he said that
del Cano was to have five hundred pieces of gold and a new
coat-of-arms. He would have his heralds design one. So before many days were over they showed del Cano a drawing
on a fine sheet of parchment. It had a globe and under it a
Latin motto which said, 'You were the first to sail around me.'

Del Cano had it engraved on everything that could be engraved, carved wherever it could be carved, and painted
wherever it could be painted.

In the meantime in Portugal, when King Manuel had heard
the news, men were busy chipping Magellan's coat-of-arms

off the stone above the door of the old house in Tras-os-
Montes. It did not hurt Magellan to have the shield with its
checked bars hacked away, and perhaps it made Manuel feel
better. There was nothing any one could do to hurt Magellan
now — nor to help him either. His wife Beatriz and Rodrigo,
his son, had both died a few months before the Victoria came
home.

Perhaps, Vasco thought, Magellan was fortunate after all.
He died knowing that he had discovered new lands for the
king who had believed in him, thinking that he had brought
true Christianity to Cebu, not knowing of the death of his
friend, of his wife, of his son.

He was spared, too, another bitter piece of knowledge.
The geographers decided, after all, that the Moluccas lay
in the Portuguese half of the world. Faleiro, who was in
prison in Portugal when the Victoria came home and who died
there soon after, had made his globe too small. The Pacific
was larger than anyone had thought. The Moluccas lay west
of the Pope's imaginary line. It ended by the Portuguese
paying Don Carlos three hundred and fifty thousand golden
ducats to forget that the western route to the Spice Islands
had been found. The sale of the cloves that the Victoria
brought home paid for the expenses of the whole voyage —
for the food and the ropes and the broken mirrors and caps
and combs and scissors and red-velvet chairs. It could not
pay for the lives of the men who had died to find the strait
and sail the Peaceful Ocean, or for those who starved till they
ate the leather off the yards or those who died wounded by
poisoned arrows ...

Still on the day that del Cano told his news and Pigafetta
presented his book and Vasco gave Don Carlos a white-
porcelain bowl with three red fishes on it, no one knew that
the Spice Islands did not lie in Spanish territory. Vasco knelt
down to show the bowl with its darting vermilion fish to the
King. He was so tall that even kneeling he did not look short.
He had sold his cloves well and the tailor had been busy

making some clothes big enough for him. He had to charge extra to make suits for giants, he said. Pigafetta was kind enough to approve of the way Vasco looked in black velvet. He had taken the rings out of his ears and his hair and beard had been trimmed. The only thing that connected him with the tattooed savage of a few days before was the gold locket that he wore on a heavy chain around his neck.

Perhaps it was some dim memory of the locket that made Don Carlos look closely at the kneeling giant with the porcelain bowl.

'I have seen you before, I think,' the King said, taking the bowl and holding it towards the light so that he could see the shadow of his fingers through the porcelain.

'Yes, Your Majesty,' Vasco said. 'I was with the Captain General when he first spoke to you about the voyage, but it is long ago now. It is wonderful that Your Majesty should remember.'

'I do not often forget a face,' the King said. 'Besides, there was something else — the locket, with my cousin's picture in it.'

'Yes, Your Majesty. It is still there.'

Vasco opened it, and the King reached for it and looked at it in silence for a moment.

'It is not badly painted,' he said, 'but I have had a better one since. The other picture I recognize, too. The young lady has been at Court with her uncle, but she returned to Portugal some months ago.'

He had answered the question that had been in Vasco's mind since they had reached Seville. So it was true: he knew no one in Spain except the crew of the Victoria, some sailors in jail for mutiny, and — this was a strange thought — the King.

It was a harsh, bare country, he thought suddenly, getting up from his knees at a sign from the King. There were too many rocks, too much blazing sunshine, too much dust and wind. Now, in Portugal there were gushing streams, roses, nightingales, music. He forgot that there were all these things too in Spain — if you knew where to look.

'What will you do now?' Don Carlos asked.

'I wish I knew,' Vasco said. 'I would go to Portugal to see my family, but King Manuel would put me in prison, I suppose. He will not be pleased with all this.'

Vasco waved his hand over the heaped treasure from the islands of the Pacific. There was a chart he had drawn of the islands. The King had the parchment in his hand and seemed to have forgotten everything else while he studied it.

At last he looked up with a smile that made his plain face charming, almost handsome.

'You might carry a message, I suppose, for me to my good brother-in-law, Don Manuel. He would hardly throw my messenger into jail.' He turned to a page who was standing near. 'Go to my room, Pedro. You will find a box wrapped in a piece of violet and gold brocade lying on the chest. Bring it to me, please.'

When the page returned with the box, Don Carlos unwrapped it and opened it. Inside was a carved and gilded frame with a picture of himself in the magnificent suit of white with the cloak of sables that he had worn at his coronation as Emperor.

'You might tell her,' Don Carlos said, 'that they always paint me even plainer than I am. Sometimes when people see me they are pleasantly surprised.'

'Tell the Princess, Your Majesty?'

Don Carlos smiled again.

'Who else? Perhaps you will be with her when she comes to Spain.'

'I am glad she is coming,' Vasco said.

He looked down at the picture again.

It was true, he thought. The King looked ugly in the picture, but he wasn't, not with those kind eyes and the understanding smile. He was a splendid king, good enough for the most beautiful princess in the world, the one in Vasco's locket.

'I — I thank Your Majesty,' he said. 'I am proud to carry it.'

Don Carlos handed him the box.

'You shall have a letter to my brother-in-law,' he said. 'The courier shall bring it to your lodgings, which are — where?'

'On the ship — the Victoria, Sire.'

'Ah — the Victoria. She was well named. I wish I could have sailed with your Captain,' the King said.

He meant it, Vasco realized. This King and Emperor was a young man, not much older than himself. He would have liked to sail to strange countries as well as the next man, but he had to spend most of his time reading dull papers and talking to duller people. Vasco remembered having heard that when he was only seven years old, Don Carlos was already signing state documents.

Del Cano had been standing like a statue all this time, but his mind was not idle. He was planning to have his new coat-of-arms embroidered on his shirts.

He made a lower bow than Vasco believed possible when the King said courteously, 'Between you and Captain Magellan, Senhor del Cano, you have won a great victory for Spain.'

They were dismissed now.

Spain, Vasco thought, as he went out, was not such a bad country after all. It had a wonderful king, and it looked as if it were going to have a queen to match.

He strode back to the Victoria with the box under his arm so fast that even del Cano had to trot to keep up with him.

MESSAGE FROM AN EMPEROR ———— 20

HE WENT to Lisbon by sea.

'Land travel is never right to a sailor,' he said. 'I would rather be drowned than breathe dust and be bitten by flies.'

'Me, I choose dust,' Pigafetta said.

He was going to France. Vasco watched him start. The last he saw of him, Pigafetta was telling a mule what he thought of him. The mule had just thrown the Knight of Rhodes into a small duck pond. It disturbed the ducks, but Pigafetta was not discouraged.

'For two maravedis I'd make stew of you, mule,' he said harshly. 'A man like me who has seen the awful things of ocean thinks little of duck ponds. Moreover, I am terrible when roused and I eat leather and broiled rats. To eat a whole mule would be nothing to me. Stand still, you miserable imitation of a Patagonian guanaco . . .'

Pigafetta brushed his wet hair out of his eyes, waved to Vasco, hit the mule — who was evidently impressed by this style of conversation — a whack and bounced off in the general direction of France. The Queen of France was charmed with him, Vasco heard later. And after all, why not?

The boat in which Vasco sailed to Lisbon was a small one. Vasco was pitched and tossed about in a storm, but most of the way the breeze was fair and they made good time. Yet this voyage from Seville to Lisbon seemed longer than the rounding of the Cape of Good Hope — or at least Vasco told Juan it did. He spent part of it telling Juan how it would be when they got there. It would still be warm in the evening. There might be a few late roses left in the garden. There would be music, and the scent of the roses would be mixed with the smell of roasting chickens and newly baked bread. Fernan would be making a stew of eight different kinds of fish with red wine in it, and there would be puddings full of fruit and spices.

'What a meal, Senhor Don Vasco! What a meal!' Juan exclaimed. 'I wish our friend, Signor Pigafetta, would be there.'

Vasco wished so too. Pigafetta would like to sit in the garden and eat chicken and joke with Vasco's pretty sisters and tell stories about birds carrying off elephants.

It was evening as the tide and the light breeze brought them at last up the Tagus. The western sky was full of bright banners of cloud, and ahead over Lisbon there was a glow of pink and pale gold. The moon was coming up out of it like a copper shield. The city seemed to hang between the river and the sky as if the breeze might blow it away.

Yet after all, the streets were solid, though they still seemed to sway beneath his feet as he hurried up the hill. The clouds had faded suddenly and it was dark in the shadow of the house. There was no light there, no music, no smell of roasting, broiling, and baking, no sound of voices from the garden.

They walked slowly through the courtyard and stood looking up at the dark door — the tall figure in the fine Spanish suit, the stubby one in rough sailor clothes that had seen both halves of the world. Vasco had bought Juan a new suit but he was saving it, he said. He used to take it out on the voyage to Lisbon and finger it respectfully. Juan had never had a new suit all at once before.

Juan had fine strong arms and shoulders. He was proud of the weight of bags and bundles he could carry. When he put them down, it made quite a heap. Vasco added his load to the pile and walked towards the great bronze door.

'Is this surely the place, Senhor Don Vasco? This very grand house to me.'

'Yes, it's the place, Juan; and remember you promised not to call me "Don." You're not a don unless your father is a marquis or a count or something. If you call me that, they'll laugh at me. And anyway in Portugal they say "Dom," not "Don."'

'Yes, Senhor D—— Senhor. You going to knock at that big door?'

There was something almost frightening about the silence. For a moment Vasco stared at the figures on the door. The moonlight was just beginning to shine into the court and he could barely make out the elephants, the dolphins, the sea shells, and the palms and spice trees.

He thought, 'Yes, they are like that,' and felt for the knocker. He knew the feeling of the twisted snakes that formed it. Its clang as it fell into place seemed to echo in emptiness.

'We'd better go and find an inn for the night, Juan,' he said at last, and stepped back towards the heaped bundles with feet that seemed suddenly too tired to move.

'That's right,' Juan said, beginning to load himself again.

He spoke cheerfully, but when Vasco was not looking, he wiped his eyes with the back of his hand. 'When people don't expect you, of course they can't always be waiting around cooking things the way we thought,' he added, slinging a heavy leather bag over his shoulder. 'While you were paying the Captain, I looked in at a tavern near the wharf. It was a nice clean place and they were going to have pancakes for supper. I heard the woman there say, "Yes, Duarte, I will make plenty of pancakes. If you will stop telling how you chased that poor young gentleman into the river," she said.'

Juan had already started out of the courtyard and Vasco was picking up the last bundle when a noise behind him made him turn.

The door of the house opened a little way, a face the same color as the door appeared through the crack and a deep voice said, 'Someone knocking loud at this door — you want something, Senhor?'

'Fernan!' Vasco shouted.

He pushed through the door and threw his arms affectionately around the big Negro.

Fernan struggled to get away, gasping: 'You man! What you doing to me? Let me go, you big gorilla!'

Vasco let him go and said laughing: 'Don't you know me, Fernan? It's Vasco. I've come home.'

'Don't know anyone eight feet tall,' Fernan grunted suspiciously. 'We had a boy named Vasco, that's true, but he was drowned long time ago other side of the world. What makes you think you him?'

'How do you suppose I know your name?'

'Everybody in Lisbon knows Fernan. I been in Lisbon before any young giant like you was born.'

'Yes, and sailed to India with my father and my Uncle Shane and cooked fish stew with eight kinds of fish, and made me honey cakes and let me ride on your shoulders and cured my finger with your good African ointment when the parrot bit it.'

'H'm,' Fernan said. 'What the name of that parrot?'

'There are two in the garden, a white cockatoo with a yellow crest and a red-and-green one. The white one bit me. His name is Melindi. The other is Calicut. They'd know me, even if you don't. Or it may be there is a red dog that remembers the night I came home bringing a wounded Malay over my shoulder: the night I gave a puppy to the Princess.'

Fernan said cautiously: 'You seem to talk as if you might be who you say you are. You tell me the name of the first red dog of all and what he did when Vasco da Gama sailed the first time to India and I'll believe you're my boy Vasco.'

Vasco gave a shrill whistle and then said, 'His name was Connemara and he swam after the ships and tried to go to India when . . .'

But before he had finished he was almost knocked down by a red dog with silky-feathery tail and paws.

'India!' Vasco said, and sat down on the ground with his dog in his arms.

India licked his face and brushed red hairs all over him. Fernan began to jump and whoop and sing. The words were in the tongue of some African tribe, but it was easy enough to understand what they meant. They meant the same thing India's wet tongue and thumping tail did — joy.

Before Fernan had stopped leaping and bounding and clapping his hands, Juan had carried in all the luggage. After a while Fernan was able to speak in Portuguese.

He was alone in the house. The family had all gone to a feast at the palace. Some of the servants had gone with them and the rest had gone to a wedding in the town.

'I stayed to take care of the house,' Fernan said, showing all his teeth in a wide grin, 'so I am the first to see my boy, Master Vasco, come home all rich and fine with a curly beard and a black slave of his own. Did they make you a duke down there in Spain, Master Vasco?'

'No, Fernan, and I'm not rich and Juan isn't my slave. He's my shipmate. We've been around the world together.'

'H'm! You too good to be a slave, black boy?'

'No — black man,' Juan said. 'I'll be Senhor D—— Senhor Vasco's slave if he likes. Of course I'll never be a fine tall man like you, but I might learn to make that grand fish stew if you'll teach me. I'm a pretty good cook now. I can make coconut cakes. First you take some coconut milk ——'

'Coconut milk! What kind of talk is that?'

'We've brought you some coconuts, Fernan. Juan will show you. I'm going to the palace.'

'To the palace? Is that your best suit? There's a masked ball there tonight. You wouldn't be dancing in those boots!'

'I have a better suit and a best suit,' Vasco said, 'and velvet shoes, though I will not dance tonight, not knowing how. But, Fernan, a feast and a masked ball in one night! Is Dom Manuel still King?'

'Yes, Master Vasco, but he has a new wife. She's the sister of the King of Spain; you know that. Things are changed up there. You put on the best suit.'

'Yes, Fernan,' Vasco said meekly.

Indeed things were changed at the palace. The windows blazed with light. Music sang out into the soft night. Vasco followed the path up the hill, the old path that he had travelled so often as a page. Branches were beginning to grow across it here and there, but it was easy to follow it in the moonlight. He found the gate he knew in the palace wall. It opened as he touched the latch. Rich smells from the kitchen met his nose. He looked in as he passed. If King Manuel could have seen the servants eating, it would have frightened him for a week.

They had left the small door unguarded and Vasco slipped through it, following remembered passages towards the music. It grew louder and he put on the black-velvet mask that Fernan had given him. There had been an extra one and someone had left it on a chair in the hall.

By the door of the room where they were dancing, two masked men were standing. They moved aside courteously to let Vasco pass. Now, a mask changes faces wonderfully, but there was no changing Shane O'Connor's red beard and hair, nor his big soft voice with its musical rise and fall.

The other man was Vasco's father. The mask could not hide from his son the way the hair grew on Joan Coelho's forehead, nor the smile that made his black brows lift, nor the square-cut emerald from India on his strong, slender hand. His hair had turned white around the temples, but this was Joan Coelho.

Vasco raised his hand to tear off his mask and speak to his father and uncle, but he let it fall again.

'It would only make a scene,' he thought. 'I'll wait for the unmasking I should have stayed at home, sent a message, I suppose.'

It made him smile as he passed them to see that these two tall men were looking up at him, not down.

Shane O'Connor and his brother-in-law, after one glance

at the young giant in violet velvet and gold, went on with their talk.

'It's a stiff kind of dancing,' Shane said. 'How the girls stand anything so dull, I can't tell. Now, in old Ireland we'd be jigging about as gay as you please and every now and then we'd give the girl a good swing, so she'd know you had a strong arm to beat her with in case she'd need it. That gives a girl good respect for a man. But this walking up and down and pointing your toes! If I wanted a walk, I'd take it in the fresh air — and the moonlight.'

'It's one of the dances the Queen brought from Spain. It's a pleasant sight, it seems to me — so many well-dressed, graceful young people. And the singing — I like the way they stop sometimes and sing to each other.'

'Squawking,' Shane said. 'There's no singing nowadays. Why, Joan, don't you remember how we sang across black boiling waves from one ship to the other? These peacocks here couldn't sing so you'd hear them across a duck pond!' He dropped his voice lower, but Vasco's sharp ears heard him add, 'Even that tall lad that came in just now probably has no more voice than a sick cricket.'

At this point Vasco felt like letting out the cry the deck boy gives when the sand has run out, but he stood still and watched the dancers.

It was, as his father had said, a pleasant sight — the gay clothes, the jewels flashing in candlelight, the feet moving so precisely to the sound of guitars, the masked faces.

'Under a mask anyone may be a beauty,' Vasco thought.

One of the ladies, he decided, must be the Queen, because King Manuel was sitting alone at the end of the room. He was not masked, but even if he had been everyone would have known him by his shabby clothes. His new Queen might make him pay for wax candles and music and fruit and wine, but she had not made him buy a new suit.

That was expecting too much, as anyone would admit, and she certainly had improved the Court. The old motheaten hangings were gone and in their place hung brilliant new tapestries. They seemed to represent Portuguese triumphs in India and Malacca and the Spice Islands, but life in these places looked cooler and more comfortable than Vasco remembered.

The dancers had paused now and the men were singing.

> 'A star fell from the sky
> And vanished from its place.
> I looked for it on high,
> But found it — in your face.'

The line of dancers formed again in a stately procession. As they passed him Vasco looked to see if he could recognize any of the masked girls. His sisters, Maria and Olivia, must be there, but he could not pick them out. The lady at the head of the line, with the green dress slashed to show primrose color with the great rope of pearls and the pendant of enormous emeralds, was probably the Queen, the sister of Don Carlos. Behind her in white must be the Princess Isabella. He knew her by her graceful way of moving and by a dimple that showed at the corner of her mask.

Far down the line red curls caught the light. Yes, that was Angela Luisa. No one could make her dancing stately. How small she looked! He looked down on the tops of all their heads — he realized — as he looked for a bush of brown curls that would be Maria da Sousa's. Only, after all, she might not be in Lisbon.

Not that it mattered where she was, of course, he told himself. He had come to Lisbon to deliver a message, and a box — he had it firmly under his arm — and to see his family. That was all.

There was a girl in yellow, taller than the others, who danced almost as well as the Princess. Her hair was brown, but it was brushed into smooth waves and braided and looped over her ears. There were ropes of seed pearls twisted in it. That was the way the Princess wore her hair, he noticed, and so did many others. They were all imitating her, no doubt.

That was the way with girls, always changing from one fashion to another.

Now they were all bowing again and the girls were singing:

'My heart is like a bird
That flies to you and sings,
And stays there, I have heard,
Because you clipped its wings.'

'That's really pretty,' Vasco heard his father say, and Shane O'Connor grumbled: 'And a sillier remark I've not often heard. If I catch any of our girls having the wings of their hearts — if they've got such things — clipped by these dancing apes, I'll have something to say, I'm telling you.'

Vasco thought, 'My uncle's right. What good would these dancers be on a ship's deck around the Cape of Storms, or eating rats on a ship in the Pacific?'

Then he heard his father say with a chuckle: 'Your own son-in-law is one of those dancing apes, Shane. Yet I believe he did fairly well in that sea fight off Malabar.'

'He's an exception,' Shane said hastily.

'Plenty of them are exceptions, then,' Joan Coelho said. 'See — it's midnight. They are going to unmask. Then we shall see who our tall friend is,' he added in a lower tone.

Now the masks were off. The mothers, aunts, and grandmothers, who were sitting on cushioned benches along the wall, took off theirs and showed how sleepy they looked. It was hard work staring through a mask all night to make sure that your daughter, niece, or granddaughter behaved properly, danced better than anyone else, and had the prettiest dress. It was especially tiring if you had to watch more than one.

The fathers, grandfathers, and uncles took off their masks and began to wonder what there would be for supper. They felt that dinner had been a long time ago.

The young men began to say to their partners, 'I knew it was you all the time,' and the girls began to tease them, saying, 'Oh, I thought you were some handsome stranger — at

least till you stepped on my foot,' or, 'Isn't Her Majesty's
dress beautiful? I hear she had it sent from Paris. And her
hair looks wonderful. I believe I'll try mine scraped off my
forehead.'

They all talked at once and swung their masks in their jewelled hands. They sounded like young swallows and looked
like birds of paradise, Vasco thought, as he stood there watching them and forgetting to take off his mask.

Yes, he was right. That was the Queen in the green slashed
dress. She looked a little like her brother, though she was
handsome and he was plain. And that was Princess Isabella,
looking lovelier than ever. Those were Angela Luisa's red
curls and that was her husband Christoval da Sousa, handsome in spite of the Moorish sword that had slashed his cheek
in the sea fight off Malabar.

But the girl in yellow had vanished somewhere in the crowd.
Vasco looked for her, quite unconscious that half the people
over whose heads he was looking were looking at him and
wondering about the tall man in violet with the package
wrapped in violet and gold under his arm.

The young escudeiro who had been dancing with the girl in
yellow walked over to Vasco. He was plump and pink and he
walked daintily, turning his toes out.

He bowed twice, like a fat thrush hopping and looking for a
worm, and then said in a high voice: 'Your pardon, Senhor.
Forgive me, Senhor. Your mask, Senhor. You are still wearing it, Senhor.'

'Why, so I am. I ask your pardon,' Vasco said, taking it
off.

The escudeiro looked up at Vasco.

'I hardly think I know you, Senhor,' he squeaked.

'I hardly think you do, Senhor,' Vasco said quietly. Then,
because he was afraid the escudeiro would burst with curiosity, he added: 'I have come from His Imperial Majesty
Don Carlos of Spain, with letters for His Majesty Dom Manuel the Fortunate, for Her Majesty Dona Leonora, and for

Her Royal Highness Dona Isabella. If you will take me to the Ambassador from Spain, I will explain to him and he will present me to His Majesty.'

'Unfortunately the Ambassador is ill. He is not here this evening. However, I can escort you to His Majesty myself. It will be quite correct.'

'Thank you,' Vasco said gravely, 'if you are sure it is correct.'

'Follow me, Senhor. You speak Portuguese very well, Senhor, if I may say so. One would think you had been born in Lisbon, Senhor.'

'Thank you. It has been necessary for me to learn several tongues,' Vasco said.

The crowd divided and let them through, the plump escudeiro tripping along and Vasco behind him, trying to shorten his stride enough not to step on his escort's heels.

It seemed to take an endless time to cross the big room. During it he saw his mother and realized that she was looking sadly at him, puzzled perhaps by a resemblance to the son she believed dead. Her hair was almost white, he saw.

Then he found himself looking down at the King. Dom Manuel looked old and tired as he listened to the escudeiro. His hand shook as he took the packet of letters from Don Carlos. He hardly glanced at Vasco, but broke the seal and glanced at the letter with his name on it.

'My brother-in-law writes long letters,' he said in his peevish voice. 'I cannot read this by candlelight. It will keep till morning, I suppose. Perhaps he writes to say that he has stolen more of my islands.'

The word 'Spain' was running through the room. The Queen and the Princess moved over to where Manuel was sitting. He thrust their letters at them and moved his hand in the sharp gesture of dismissal that Vasco remembered.

'You may leave us,' Manuel said curtly.

'Forgive me, Your Majesty,' Vasco said. 'I was commanded by the King of Spain to give this' — he held out the violet wrapped box — 'into the hands of Her Royal Highness. There is also a message.'

He remembered how you offered things to a princess. You stooped forward, turned out one foot, put the other hand back of you, held out whatever it was far enough so that she need not move from her place. You bent the knee, and after she had taken whatever you were holding, you put your right hand over your heart, bowed yourself a step backwards.

Yes — that was it, and now she had the bundle in her hands and was undoing the velvet wrapping.

'There was a message, you said. Deliver it — deliver it!' Manuel said impatiently.

The Princess had opened the box and was looking at the picture.

'His Majesty Don Carlos said I was to say to Her Royal Highness that painters often make him look uglier than he is. He says that when people see him, they are often so surprised that they think he is quite handsome.'

The Queen laughed.

'Ah, that is like Carlos,' she said. 'I can hear his voice saying it. May I see the picture, dearest? Oh! How stiff and furiously solemn he looks in his best clothes! Dear Carlos — there isn't a man like him. He's such a mixture. He's as brave as a lion and afraid of spiders — and mice. He knows more law than the lawyers and more of war than the generals, but he is the happiest playing the flute or watching a sparrow build her nest or inventing a clock. He is the most generous man in the world and always takes an old cloak along to protect his best one.'

'Sensible fellow,' Manuel said approvingly.

'One day,' the Queen went on, 'he was talking to an old peasant who did not know he was speaking to the King. He scolded Carlos because the crops were so poor and times so bad. Then some of Carlos's escort came up and the man knew it was the King. He did not take back any of his cross words. He just grinned and said, "If I'd known it was you, I'd have said twice as much."

'The courtiers were shocked, but Carlos just laughed. He gave the man fifty ducats, someone told me. He's wonderful even if he is plain.'

'I think he's splendid-looking,' the Princess said.

'Crazy,' Manuel said, but whether he was talking about a king who, in spite of his care of his best clothes, would give away fifty ducats or about his daughter's admiration of the picture was not clear.

While the Queen had been speaking Manuel had been looking Vasco up and down, all six feet four of him.

'I suppose you are one of those big-footed giants my brother-in-law's ships brought back when they came from stealing my spices,' he said with a snigger. 'I suppose they call you Senhor Patagonia.'

'If Your Majesty says so,' Vasco said courteously, although he was getting a little tired of this joke.

Princess Isabella put the picture back in its box and said to her father: 'I think our guests are waiting. They were to dance one more before supper. I will find a partner for this gentleman.'

Vasco blushed.

'I don't dance, Your Royal Highness.'

'From Spain? And you don't dance! Oh, that's impossible. You have watched this dance. You must see that anyone can do it who can walk. My lady-in-waiting here is an excellent teacher.'

She stepped forward and Vasco followed her. Suddenly he saw a yellow dress and brown hair with pearls twisted in it. He found himself looking down at Maria da Sousa. The pink puff ball of an escudeiro was standing beside her.

He looked like a cross baby when the Princess said: 'Maria, this gentleman, Senhor — Patagonia has come from Spain with messages from His Imperial Majesty. Will you dance with him and see that he is well entertained at supper? Dona Maria da Sousa will take care of you, Senhor.'

'I'm afraid I don't know this dance,' Vasco said, when the

Princess had gone and the escudeiro after six or seven bows had left them to escort her across the room.

'You need only walk by my side and turn when I tell you to,' Maria said. 'What did you say to the Marquis to make him look as if he had swallowed a chestnut — with the burr still on?'

'So that pink piglet is a marquis,' Vasco thought. 'Well, it takes all kinds of people to make a nobility.'

He answered Maria by saying: 'He did most of the talking — and all the walking on tiptoe. Shall I call him back?'

'Try it and see what happens,' Maria da Sousa said.

Vasco looked down at her and realized suddenly that she was beautiful. Her skin was like the lining of a sea shell. Her hair rippled like sand after the waves had run away. The candle-light caught the gold on the edges of the ripples. Her eyes were like the sunshine dancing on water. When she spoke it was like a fair breeze coming up after a hot calm.

He was still busy thinking thoughts a sailor thinks when the music began. Yes, it was time. She moved like a wave or like a ship under full sail, going through a blue strait with a light wind and a whispering tide.

Somehow Vasco found himself dancing and without stepping on anyone's feet — except his own.

When the dancers stopped he found himself singing with the other men.

'A star fell from the sky...'

The dancing began again. Above the music Vasco heard Maria say, 'I like to hear you sing, Vasco.'

'You — you knew me!' he said, looking down and almost stumbling.

'Not till you took your mask off — no, turn this way — but even if you hadn't, it wouldn't have been very hard to know you. Not with my picture and the Princess's hanging around your neck.'

Vasco looked down at the locket. It was hanging open.

'Did she know me too? Did she bring me to you, because she knew?'

'Was the Princess ever stupid — Senhor Patagonia?' She was laughing. 'You are too tall to see what goes on down here. Oh, Vasco. I'm so glad you weren't drowned. We wouldn't believe it, Angela Luisa and the Princess and I, even when all the others did. But it's been so long waiting — no, turn left and stand still, while I sing . . .

'My heart is like a bird . . .'

'You must tell your family now,' Maria said when the dancing was over.

'Not here,' Vasco said. 'Not with all these people looking on.'

'Go into the little room where the pages take their lessons. I'll tell Angela and they'll soon be there.'

So it was in that dingy little room where he had been switched for ignorance of French that Vasco saw his family again. They were around him, laughing, crying, kissing him, thumping his shoulders — those who could reach them, all talking at once.

Even Abraham, that model young man, was quite impressed when he found out how many cloves Vasco had sold in Seville. Abraham never had to count on his fingers to see whether you were worth knowing. He could figure instantly.

Vasco thought Abraham was growing to look like a king — King Manuel, in fact.

They left the supper, although as Queen Leonora had ordered it, it was a good supper, and went home.

Maria went with them.

'Since my uncle died,' she told him, 'I live with your family when I am not at Court.'

'I know a short cut,' Vasco said.

Somehow every one else had followed the main road. The path did not prove to be a very short cut. The marble bench was still there — the bench where Magellan had sat on the day when King Manuel had dismissed him because he asked for a milreis a day.

The bench was in shadow, but the moon was silvering the world outside. They sat there while Vasco told her about

Magellan's grim courage, his patience, his hour of triumph, his death.

Vasco felt less sad when he had told her about it because he saw her crying. No one else had cared.

'Tell me more about the voyage — about yourself,' she said after a while.

'There'll be time for that later.'

'How much time?'

'All my life, I hope,' Vasco said.

Fernan had been busy. He had been cooking. So had Juan. He had been baking coconut cakes. He had also been slicing onions, boning fish, chopping chicken livers, stoning olives, and in fact jumping to do whatever Fernan told him.

'Thirty, forty years, you'll make a pretty good cook,' Fernan said encouragingly. 'Now you carry in that bowl of sauce. If you spill it, I put you on my spit and roast you. See?'

'Yes, Senhor Fernan. I'll be the most careful black boy ever was in this kitchen.'

'Now tell me who are all those people,' Juan said when he came back.

'Well, that tall lady with the black hair, that's Master Vasco's Aunt Luisa. And the two young men that look a little like Master Vasco, they're her sons. Dennis and Paulo O'Connor are their names.'

'Who is the lady with the red curls who teases everyone?'

'That is their sister — Countess da Sousa, but I always call her Dona Angela myself. That is her husband with the scar on his face. Some Moorish pirate did that.'

'Malay pirates are worse,' Juan said. 'They're mean. Why when I was in the Moluccas ——'

'Black boy,' Fernan said solemnly, 'I knew how mean those Malays could be when you were just a monkey hanging by your tail from a palm tree. Now, you see that big man with the red whiskers?'

'The one playing the harp?'

'You see anyone else with red whiskers? Yes, that's Senhor Shane O'Connor, who came out of Ireland and talks all the while about how grand it is but never goes back there.'

'Is he — Senhor Vasco's uncle?'

'Yes, and remember your manners, black boy. You must call him Dom Vasco now.'

Juan hung his jaw open.

'I must? You mean he's a lord all the time?'

'It just happens he might not know it,' Fernan said. 'You see that tall gentleman in black? Well, that's Master Vasco's father. King Manuel, he made him a marquis and he's Dom Joan Coelho now. And the little lady with the white hair is his wife, Dona Rachel. Those two pretty young ladies, one in pink, one in blue, are Master Vasco's sisters — Dom Vasco to you. Think you can remember that?'

'Yes, I think so,' Juan chuckled. 'I certainly think so.'

'Well, those two ladies are married now, but their husbands are in India, serving under da Gama. He's the Viceroy there now. You don't need to learn their names. Just say "Yes, my lady" and "No, my lady" if they speak to you. Understand that?'

'Yes, Senhor Fernan. And there's a skinny gentleman who keeps saying, "Strange Vasco does not come, most inconsiderate," and snapping his fingers. He told me not to light the candles too soon. It would waste wax, he said.'

'That's Master Vasco's brother, Dom Abraham.'

'Glad he's not my brother,' Juan said, grinning.

'Dom Abraham is one of The Family,' Fernan said coldly. 'You carry in the olives now, and I'll take in the fish stew. That suit Master Vasco bought you fits you all right. I like that dark ruby color on you. Just you behave as well as you look, now ...'

Dom Abraham Coelho found his father and his Uncle Shane sitting together at the end of the big room. They were not talking, just sitting quietly together watching their families enjoy themselves. The big room was full of people. Fernan had not named more than half of them. Shane had put down his harp and was feeling the ears of the red Irish dog, who had her head on his knee.

'India, good dog, India,' he murmured from time to time.

Abraham's voice interrupted this comfortable time.

'Since you have nothing to do just now, Father, I should like to speak to you.'

'Certainly, Abraham,' Joan Coelho said.

He wondered what Abraham was going to scold him about now. Joan tried hard to remember that he was the head of the family and that when he gave the new chapel to the church King Manuel had made him a marquis 'for his services to Church and State.' Somehow Abraham always made him feel that he was a small boy who had been caught stealing honey with the honey all over his face.

'We discussed at one time the desirability of a marriage between me and Dona Maria da Sousa,' Abraham began in his careful way.

'Lovely girl,' Shane O'Connor said. 'Like a wild rose.'

'Her dowry is considerable,' Abraham went on, 'and as you are her guardian it seemed a suitable arrangement.' Abraham always chose the longer of two words if there were two that would do. 'I had your permission to address her, but having done so, on more than one occasion, I have come to the conclusion that she is — flighty.'

'That's bad, very bad,' Shane said, shaking his head solemnly. 'That a young girl would be flighty! Think of that, now!'

'It has come to my attention,' Abraham went on, without apparently noticing that he and his uncle lived on the same planet, 'that Dona Anna da Castro is also fittingly dowered. She seems like a serious young woman and it has been indicated to me that her father would be pleased with such an alliance.'

'There's one marriage you won't need to tire yourself arranging. By the look of it, I'd say it has been arranged already.'

'An alliance — that sounds fine, now,' murmured Shane. 'Doesn't it, now, India, good dog?'

'But of course,' Abraham went on, 'I would not choose to do anything incorrect. If you consider my honor pledged to Dona Maria, I will, of course, redeem it. Only, it occurred to me that as Vasco has now returned, perhaps a marriage could be arranged between them, and her dowry ——'

'Would be kept in the family. Yes, I understand you, Abraham. I think you may feel free. I will speak to Senhor de Castro soon. Tomorrow, perhaps. And do not worry about Maria. She will have plenty of suitors. And indeed I am a little tired of arranging marriages. Just when the girls grow up and are attractive, I seem to give them away to someone else. But you will bring Dona Anna home. That will be pleasant. We shall welcome her gladly.'

'Thank you, Father,' Abraham said.

'I wonder what made me think of cold buttermilk,' Shane said when Abraham had departed to count the wine jugs and snuff the candles.

'He's a good boy, Shane,' Joan Coelho said. 'Honest. Sensible. Hard working. Kind to his mother.'

'Who wouldn't be? That's no hard work,' Shane grumbled. 'Quiet now, Star of India. What, you'd leave me, would you?'

The footsteps were Vasco's and Maria's.

'I think,' said Shane O'Connor, watching their happy faces as they bent over the red dog, 'there's one marriage you won't need to tire yourself arranging. By the look of it, I'd say it has been arranged already.'

THE END